"I do believe the best peach I ever ate in my life I had in Georgia on the Fourth of July in '64."

A quick anger stilled the flutters inside Charity. She thought of the times she'd seen Yankee soldiers stroll through the Georgia countryside picking fruit indiscriminately, as if such acts of trespassing were their right. Lifting her chin, she fixed Daniel with a stony stare and pasted on a stilted smile. "I wonder, sir, from whose orchard you stole that memorable piece of fruit?"

"Charity!" Aunt Jennie hissed from one end of the table, while Uncle Silas harrumphed from the other.

But Daniel never flinched. His gaze remained fixed to Charity's face. "Actually, Miss Langdon," he said, directing his reply to her as if Silas and Jennie Gant were not in the room, "the peach was a gift."

RAMONA K. CECIL is a wife, mother, grandmother, freelance poet, and award-winning inspirational romance writer. Now empty nesters, she and her husband make their home in Indiana. A member of American Christian Fiction Writers and American Christian Fiction Writers Indiana Chapter, her work has won awards in a number of inspirational writing contests. Over eighty of her inspirational verses have been published on a wide array of items for the Christian gift market. Through her speaking ministry, she enjoys encouraging aspiring writers by sharing her story of how she became a published author. When not writing, her hobbies include reading, gardening, and visiting places of historical interest.

Books by Ramona K. Cecil

HEARTSONG PRESENTS
HP792—Sweet Forever
HP812—Everlasting Promise

B

Charity's
Heart

Ramona K. Cecil

Heartsong Presents

Special thanks to the Jennings County Historical Society of Vernon, Indiana; Ron Grimes, Archivist at the Jefferson County Historical Society of Madison, Indiana; and my husband, Jim, and daughters, Jennifer and Kelly, for their love, encouragement, and support.

A note from the Author:
I love to hear from my readers! You may correspond with me by writing:

Ramona K. Cecil
Author Relations
PO Box 721
Uhrichsville, OH 44683

ISBN 978-1-60260-266-3

CHARITY'S HEART

All scripture quotations are taken from the King James Version of the Bible.

All of the characters and events in this book are fictitious. Any resemblance to actual persons, living or dead, or to actual events is purely coincidental.

Our mission is to publish and distribute inspirational products offering exceptional value and biblical encouragement to the masses.

PRINTED IN THE U.S.A.

one

"Are you a bummer, Mr. Morgan? Because I must warn you, my Uncle Silas does not abide bummers."

Charity Langdon fought to keep her voice coolly aloof and to maintain her unflinching gaze on the man's dark eyes. She must not allow this Yankee—whose considerable height and broad shoulders filled the narrow doorway—the satisfaction of knowing his presence intimidated her.

"No ma'am." He stepped nearer her desk in the corner of the mill. The limp she'd noticed when he first walked in seemed even more pronounced, and she stifled a frustrated sigh. How many wounded Yankee veterans—transients really—had come through the doors of her uncle's grist and sawmill this past summer only to work a week or two and then disappear?

The man, who'd moments earlier introduced himself as Daniel Morgan, fished in the pocket of his faded blue calico shirt and pulled out a crumpled scrap of newspaper. He held it out. "I'm responding to the advertisement for a mill foreman Mr. Gant placed in the *Plain Dealer*."

Charity's gaze roved unbidden down the length of the stranger. Something uncomfortable twanged in her midsection. She had to grudgingly admit that with his strong, clean-shaven jaw, thick shock of dark hair, and muscular form clad in calico shirt and cotton work trousers, he was more than passably good-looking.

The hint of a smile quirked up the corner of his mouth as his dark gaze smoldered into hers. He'd noticed her appraisal!

Heat leapt to her cheeks. Feeling like a cat that had just

been caught with cream on its whiskers, she snatched the bit of grimy paper from his fingers. With an impatient whirl, she turned toward the open window as if to better catch the rays of the late August afternoon sun and pretended to read the small square of newsprint. In truth, she'd written the thing herself and knew its contents well.

When she felt her features had sufficiently cooled, she delicately cleared her throat and turned back to Daniel Morgan. "Have you any experience in the workin's of a grist mill, Mr. Morgan? The notice states plainly that the successful applicant must have at least two years'—"

"Yes, ma'am." For some reason, his eager answer, abruptly cutting short her caution, didn't bother her as much as she would have expected. "Before the war, I spent three years working at Kendall's Mill on Crooked Creek," he said without a blink. "It had a combination grist and sawmill operation, too. The last year I was there—in '61—I worked as foreman."

"I see." Charity didn't doubt the man could well fill the position of foreman, but the uneasy feeling he caused inside her made her search for a reason to send him on his way. "Well, Mr. Morgan," she said, her voice slightly diminished, "my uncle is not here right now, and I do not have the authority to hire."

She turned and rounded her desk, willing him to leave. Somehow, it was too easy to see this man in the dark blue uniform of a Union soldier. Why, he could even have been among General Sherman's army that forced her to flee her home in Georgia and take refuge up here in Indiana with Aunt Jennie and Uncle Silas.

Perhaps when he left, the tightness around her middle would relax and she could go back to ciphering the figures in her ledger book. She could always depend upon getting blissfully lost in the numbers. Seating herself behind the desk, she reached for a pencil and nearly jumped when he touched the back of her hand.

"How dare you, sir!" She jerked her hand away from his

touch as if she'd been burned. For one awful instant, the vision of another tall Union soldier grasping her hand flashed before her mind's eye. She fought to control her erratic breathing.

"I beg your pardon." His face flushed a ruddy hue beneath his tanned skin. "I should have asked your permission. I meant no offense. I just noticed your wound and was concerned it might be infected."

She glanced down at the ragged-edged red streak running diagonally across the back of her hand. Yesterday, while walking past a pile of lumber, she'd raked her hand against the splintered end of a board and scratched it deeply. "It's just a scratch. It will heal." She managed to regain her composure but again felt heat tingle in her cheeks.

"You should bind it with a clean cloth soaked in a diluted carbolic acid solution."

At his odd suggestion, she swung her gaze up from her injury to meet his handsome face, which was full of concern. The caring look touched her and she tempered her voice. "Are you a doctor?" What kind of man comes into a mill looking for work then offers medical advice?

He shook his head, and she noticed how his hair looked almost blue-black in the shaft of sunlight slanting through the open window behind her. "No, but my pa is a doctor. A few months ago, he read about an English surgeon who's been treating wounds that way to prevent infection. Pa's started using the treatment in his practice down in Madison and says it seems to work."

The *whoosh* of running water followed by the groaning of timbers and the sound of stone grinding against stone told her old Charlie Brewster had opened the sluice gate. The big wheel outside her window, which powered the mechanisms inside the mill, began turning. She was glad for the noise that hampered further conversation with this troubling man.

"Can I help you, sir?" Uncle Silas's deep, booming voice carried across the dusty mill, sending a measure of relief through

Charity. Now her uncle could deal with the man.

The applicant gave her a cursory smile and nod of his head. Then he turned to her uncle, who ushered him outside, Charity assumed, to prevent their words from being drowned by the cacophony of the mill.

Despite Charity's efforts to concentrate on adding the debit column in her ledger book, her gaze kept drifting upward and out the open door where Uncle Silas stood talking with the tall Yankee.

A disquieting sensation tingled inside her. Anticipation? Trepidation? She wasn't sure which. This Daniel Morgan didn't look, talk, or act like any other mill worker she'd known. Well-groomed, well-spoken, and obviously intelligent, he seemed as if he would fit much neater into his father's profession of physician than that of a mill worker.

Thankfully, Uncle Silas was very choosy about whom he hired. Most likely, as he had done several times this past week, he would shake his head and send the man on his way.

But when she looked up again after trying unsuccessfully to add a column of numbers she could have normally ciphered in her sleep, Charity felt as if a swarm of butterflies fluttered about in her stomach. Uncle Silas was smiling and pumping the tall, dark-haired Yankee's hand.

~

Gasping for breath, Daniel sat straight up in bed. His heart hammered like a triple-time drum cadence. He pushed his hair away from his sweaty forehead and willed his eyes to focus in the dim light.

Gratefully sucking in gulps of air, he realized he wasn't on the *Sultana* but in the neat little upstairs bedroom he'd rented at Essie Kilgore's boardinghouse in Vernon. His heart began to slow to a more normal speed, and he pushed away the covers. The mattress squeaked as he swung his unsteady legs over its side.

Rising, he half stumbled to the open window. He inhaled

the warm, honeysuckle-scented evening breeze that gently rustled the leaves of the poplar tree outside his window. The pleasant, familiar smells and sounds calmed him, coaxing him more fully awake and distancing him from the terrifying images that had haunted his sleep.

Embarrassment, disgust, and anger tangled inside him.

He turned back to the moonlight-dappled room. His bare feet padded on the smooth, varnished floorboards as he crossed to the little washstand. With steadier hands than he'd had a few moments earlier, he lifted the water pitcher and poured himself a glass of the tepid liquid. There was something reassuring in knowing he was in control of the water flowing down his throat.

He returned to his bed and strove to discover what had initiated his latest nightmare. The dreams always carried sickening similarities. Watching Fred and Tom being beaten to death in the sewage-fouled mud of Andersonville. Reliving his futile effort to come to their aid. Feeling the whack of the iron rod against his lower left leg, snapping it like a matchstick. Hearing the hateful laughter of the prison guard who'd swung the rod. Then battling for his life in the dark, muddy waters of the Mississippi River and watching "Ol' Miss" swallow down the flaming ruins of the *Sultana* like a fire-eater at the circus.

It had been at least a month since nightmares forced him to relive the horrors of the Confederate prisoner-of-war camp and the explosion of the steamboat that had carried him homeward after the war. He'd come to Vernon to get a new start—to help put the nightmares behind him. So what had triggered this latest episode?

In an effort to scour the terrifying scenes from his mind, he tried to focus on more pleasant thoughts. The vision of an angelic face, hair the color of sun-ripened wheat, and pale blue eyes the shade of an August sky assembled themselves in his mind. Warmth spread through him. His new boss's niece and bookkeeper had been a delightful surprise. Knowing he would be seeing her each day, Daniel doubted Silas Gant would ever find him late to work.

Wishing he had a name to put with her face, he scrubbed his still damp forehead with his hand. He was sure Silas Gant had mentioned his niece's name when he'd agreed to hire him.

"Glad to welcome you to Gant's Sawmill, son. I'll have Charity fill out the paperwork."

Charity. Daniel had a name to attach to her features.

He eased himself back onto the bed, pulled the covers to his chin, and expelled a soft sigh as he allowed his head to sink into the goose-down pillow.

"Charity," he whispered to the dark room, trying out the name on his tongue.

Suddenly, an uneasy feeling gripped his chest as he remembered her voice—slow and smooth as molasses. Her thick Southern drawl echoed the same enunciations as his torturers in Andersonville.

The smile that had touched his lips at the memory of the blond beauty at Gant's Mill evaporated. Daniel knew what had brought about his latest nightmare.

two

"Pearl, please set an extra place at the dinner table as we will be having a guest."

Charity stopped stirring the pot of chicken and noodles when she heard Aunt Jennie's voice coming from the kitchen doorway. She turned from the stove in time to see the house-maid nod her dark, kerchief-clad head in obedience.

Charity was not surprised to learn that someone would be joining them for dinner. Aunt Jennie loved company, and a Sunday rarely passed without at least one guest at the table. She reached halfway up the stovepipe and gave the damper a quarter turn. With another diner coming, they couldn't afford to burn anything.

She turned toward her aunt. "Who are we entertainin' today, Aunt Jennie? Surely it cannot be our turn so soon again to host Reverend Davenport?"

Aunt Jennie gingerly lifted her black silk bonnet from her salt-and-pepper hair. "No." She smoothed back a few errant strands of hair that had pulled free of the chignon at the back of her head. "It's young Mr. Morgan—Silas's new mill foreman."

Charity's heart skipped a beat. When she found sufficient breath to speak, she strove to keep her voice casual. "Do you think that is wise, Aunt Jennie? After all, he is little more than a stranger." She went back to stirring and prodding things on the stove that required no attention.

In the four days since he'd come to work at her uncle's mill, Charity had continued to feel disconcerted when Daniel Morgan was near. So far, she had managed to maintain her distance from him, having only brief contact when he brought her the work orders from which she wrote customers' bills. Beyond murmured pleasantries, their conversation had been limited strictly to business matters. So the thought of exchanging dinner conversation with this former Yankee soldier was less than palatable.

An audible sigh heaved Aunt Jennie's plump, black bombazine–clad form. She fixed Charity with that patronizing, near-pitying look that always scraped down her last nerve. Aunt Jennie never seemed to take seriously any of the accounts of Yankee treachery Charity had shared with her aunt since Charity's arrival in Vernon, Indiana, nearly two years ago. "I'm sure there is nothing to fear from Mr. Morgan, Charity. Your Uncle Silas is a great judge of character, and he has only praise for the young man."

Aunt Jennie turned her attention to her bonnet and brushed at some perceived blemish. "Besides," she added with a slight upward tilt of her chin, "I've come to learn that my dear friend Iris Pemberton's second cousin once removed has been a patient of Mr. Morgan's father for years now." Her gray eyes pinned Charity with a look as immovable as the granite they resembled. "Mr. Morgan comes from a *very* good family." As if to pronounce an end to the conversation, Aunt Jennie turned and left the kitchen.

Now Charity understood the invitation. Aunt Jennie was always alert to any connections that might serve to elevate her socially.

Pearl entered the kitchen from the dining room, a toothy grin shining from the midst of her dusky features. "Mmmm, mmmm! Haven't seen you this befuddled since Granger Hardwick showed up on yer mamma's porch with a fist full o' roses an' magnolia blossoms!"

"Pearl Emanuel! Don't you dare mention Granger in the same breath as that—that Yankee!" Charity whirled on her childhood friend and confidante. For once, she wished Pearl wasn't so attuned to her emotions.

Pearl cocked her head, obviously unfazed by Charity's rebuke. "Miss Charity, you know I can always tell what's goin' on inside you." She began scrubbing the kitchen worktable, washing away the remnants of her earlier noodle-making. As she worked, her dark eyes flashed upward glances toward Charity. "I didn't breathe nothin' 'bout no Yankee and you know it!"

The familiar little pain stabbed inside Charity at the mention of her dead fiancé, but she was surprised at how blunted it had become. "You know very well what I mean!" She kept her face averted from Pearl's. "I just don't like the idea of a Yankee soldier—"

Pearl shook her head. "Mr. Morgan ain't no soldier no more. 'Sides, Jesus tells us we got to love our enemies."

Charity winced at Pearl's words. The Bible had been her primer. She knew Christ's teachings concerning forgiveness and turning the other cheek as well as Pearl knew them. Every Sunday from the pulpit, Reverend Davenport preached about healing, about "binding up the country's wounds," as Mr. Lincoln had said in his last inaugural speech.

And Charity had made a conscious effort to do just that. In April of last year, she'd wept when she learned of Mr. Lincoln's death at the hand of an assassin, sensing the slain president had genuinely cared for the suffering South as much as for those who'd suffered above the Mason-Dixon Line.

This past spring, she'd joined a sizable group of Christian ladies from the community to place flowers on the graves of Union soldiers. She hoped, in her absence, others were decorating the final resting places of Granger and her brother, Asa. But after all she'd seen, all she'd been through, all she'd lost, Charity had begun to wonder if complete forgiveness was even possible.

A mischievous glint sparked from Pearl's dark eyes. "Joy Rose Nash says she went with her man Ned to take a load o' corn down there to the mill a few days ago. Says she done seen the new foreman and he's a real looker."

At Pearl's comment, Daniel Morgan's image came into focus in Charity's mind, and she felt her cheeks tingle warmly. She turned away from Pearl's teasing grin. "All I know is he once wore Yankee blue. And I find the thought of sittin' directly across the table from a man whose minie ball might have killed Granger or Asa distasteful!"

An hour later, as the party gathered in the dining room for Sunday dinner, Charity had to remind herself of her earlier declaration to Pearl. Indeed, she could find little distasteful about Daniel Morgan's appearance. Having seen him only in his coarse work clothes, she had to admit in his black serge suit, starched white shirt, and black silk string tie he cut quite a dashing figure.

Charity willed her hands not to tremble as she adjusted the folds of her blue-striped silk skirt around the seat of the cherry-wood dining chair. She managed to murmur her thanks as Daniel held her chair then helped her to scoot it up to the table.

With Aunt Jennie and Uncle Silas occupying the opposite ends of the rectangular table, she and Daniel were relegated to staring directly across its narrow breadth at one another. Thankfully, the moment Uncle Silas finished saying grace, he opened the conversation with talk of the mill.

Charity pushed her chicken and noodles around her plate and tried to avert her gaze from Daniel Morgan's hypnotically dark eyes. But she found herself repeatedly studying his handsome features. Invariably, whenever her gaze drifted to his face, she would be met by his gentle smile and a lingering look that set her heart fluttering.

During the main course, she managed to say little as her aunt and uncle peppered Daniel with questions about his family in Madison and his past experience in mill work.

Aunt Jennie sipped from her water goblet then daintily touched her linen napkin to her lips. "I trust, young man, that you are not related to the infamous General Morgan of the

Confederacy who brought the war to our very porch steps?"

Daniel grinned and gave a little shake of his head. "Not as far as I know. My father's people hail from the Shay's Mill area in Washington County." He managed to sneak a bite between sentences. "My uncles and cousins still run the grist mill there that my grandfather built back in 1820."

Watching his impeccable manners and good-natured temper amid her aunt's and uncle's relentless barrage of questions, Charity noticed that her feelings toward Daniel Morgan had softened. Pearl's earlier comment pricked her conscience. The War, indeed, was over. So the man had fought on the side of the Yankees. Chances were he had never been near Asa or Granger.

Lost in her muse, Charity scarcely noticed Pearl enter the dining room bearing a tray laden with slices of the pie Charity had made yesterday.

Uncle Silas's voice filtered through Charity's thoughts. "Thank you, Pearl. I always save room for desert. And there's nothing better than Charity's wonderful peach pie."

As Pearl served the pie, her glance flitted between Charity and Daniel, and her left eyebrow shot up. She sent Charity a sly, teasing grin.

The wings of the butterflies in Charity's stomach beat harder, fanning new flames in her cheeks. She sent Pearl a warning glare.

A mischievous twinkle danced in Pearl's eyes as she served Daniel a slice.

After a quick, murmured thanks to Pearl, Daniel Morgan's lips tipped up and his gaze turned to capture Charity's. "I do believe the best peach I ever ate in my life I had in Georgia on the Fourth of July in '64."

A quick anger stilled the flutters inside Charity. She thought of the times she'd seen Yankee soldiers stroll through the Georgia countryside picking fruit indiscriminately, as if such acts of trespassing were their right. Lifting her chin, she fixed Daniel with a stony stare and pasted on a stilted smile. "I wonder, sir, from whose orchard you stole that memorable piece of fruit?"

"Charity!" Aunt Jennie hissed from one end of the table, while Uncle Silas harrumphed from the other.

But Daniel never flinched. His gaze remained fixed to Charity's face. "Actually, Miss Langdon," he said, directing his reply to her as if Silas and Jennie Gant were not in the room, "the peach was a gift." He went on to tell how he and his troop of soldiers had passed a slave boy wheeling a barrow far too large for him to manage down a dusty road on the hot July day. The boy offered each soldier a peach, thus considerably lightening his load.

Shame burned hot on Charity's face. The words from the Gospel of Luke Reverend Davenport had read from the pulpit this morning replayed through her mind. *Judge not, and ye shall not be judged: condemn not, and ye shall not be condemned: forgive, and ye shall be forgiven.*

Charity opened her mouth to speak and her voice squeaked. She cleared her throat and began again in a low, penitent tone, not quite managing to meet his eyes. "Please forgive my impertinence and bad manners, sir. I fear I have sinned against you and our Lord."

"Not at all, dear lady. I'm sad to say your assumption was far too often the situation. Our army did not always show respect for the property of the Southern citizens." His gentle smile and soft voice disarmed Charity, causing her to swallow the renegade tears threatening to well in her eyes.

But from somewhere back in her mind, an insidious voice rasped, *He was in Georgia in July of 1864.* Daniel Morgan could very well have faced Asa and Granger across the battleground of Peachtree Creek.

❧

Daniel stood by the pile of freshly sawed lumber. Using the top piece as a writing surface, he scribbled figures on the customer's bill, but his mind refused to focus on his ciphering.

The memory of Charity Langdon's blue eyes glistening with tears across the Gants' dinner table would not let him be.

Sighing, he lifted his gaze from the scrap of paper and looked out over the Muscatatuck River, winding its way through the dense woods that edged it. He'd come here to forget the war—forget all the trespasses committed against him as well as the trespasses he'd committed against others. But after three sleepless nights, he'd come to the painful conclusion that Charity Langdon would never allow him to do that.

He scrubbed his face with his hand. The girl had a hold on him. Her image owned his first thoughts upon awakening and his last upon repose. But to stay would only ensure deeper heartache, and that was something he could well do without. Her accusation at the Sunday dinner table had made it clear that she held a low opinion of those who'd worn the Union blue. Daniel wondered if it would be wise—or even possible—to attempt to bridge the chasm that seemed to separate them.

Daniel snatched the invoice from the piece of lumber. A quick anger shot through him. He liked this sawmill. He liked working for Silas Gant. And in the short time he'd been here, he, Silas, and Charlie Brewster had become an almost seamless working team.

His heart thumped harder with each step toward Charity's little office. She had crawled under his skin and bored into his heart like no other woman—even Phoebe.

He'd been surprised at how quickly after enlisting in the army his heartache over his former fiancée's rejection had dissipated. In hindsight, he'd seen that theirs would have been a miserable union. By breaking their engagement and marrying that banker, Phoebe had done them both a great favor.

As he neared Charity's desk, he saw her honey-colored head bent over the ledger book. She lifted her lovely face and Daniel's heart bucked.

What sin have I done that God should dangle one so fair, yet unobtainable, before me?

He swallowed, attempting to moisten his dry throat. He held the invoice out toward her. "Here is the invoice for the lumber we sawed for Ed Cochrane. He's waiting out front. Soon as you've recorded the amount, I'll take it to him."

"Thank you, Mr. Morgan." She accepted the invoice with a quick, almost shy smile. Since Sunday, he'd noticed her mood had turned markedly quiet and reserved. She scanned the invoice, and her delicate brow knitted together in a concerned look. Her pink rosebud lips formed an O.

Suddenly, the worry lines vanished from her forehead. She smiled up at him—a sweet smile that warmed him all the way to his heart. "You may go help Mr. Cochrane load up his lumber, Mr. Morgan, but don't quote him an amount. Just tell him I will be out with the invoice shortly."

Although a bit bemused, Daniel obeyed. Besides being his boss's niece, Charity Langdon was the prettiest thing he'd ever had the pleasure of gazing upon. He reckoned he'd do just about anything she might ask of him.

A few minutes later when Charity emerged from the mill, Daniel paused in loading Ed Cochrane's lumber.

With a bright smile, she handed Daniel a different piece of paper from the one he'd figured. "Mr. Morgan, I have prepared Mr. Cochrane's invoice as you asked."

Daniel scanned the invoice and his heart nearly stopped. His original figures would have shorted the sawmill by twenty-five percent.

He jerked his face up to Charity's, and their gazes locked. He swallowed hard at the unmistakable message he read in her pretty blue eyes. She would never breathe a word of his mistake.

With a less than steady hand, he passed the invoice to Ed Cochrane, who nodded and followed Charity into the mill to settle his debt. Daniel watched the two disappear into the building and knew that Charity Langdon had just saved his job.

Something squeezed hard inside his chest. Good sense told him it was folly to stay. But after what she'd just done for him, he knew he couldn't leave Vernon, or Gant's Mill. He would regret it for the rest of his life if he didn't at least try to win Charity's heart.

three

Pearl's familiar three taps sounded on Charity's bedroom door, bringing Charity out of her bed.

When Charity opened the door, Pearl sashayed into the room carrying a steaming pitcher and humming a happy tune.

"What has put you in such a bright mood this mornin'?" Charity smiled as she quickly changed from her nightdress into bloomers and a camisole.

Though always a happy soul, Pearl seemed especially chipper. She set the pitcher of hot water on the washstand. "Miz Gant jist said I could take a few days off to go visit Mammy and Pappy down in Madison."

Pearl's news rasped against Charity's conscience. She knew Pearl missed her folks. Yet Charity was thankful that her childhood friend, who'd been more like a sister to her than a slave during their growing up years in Georgia, had chosen to come work for Aunt Jennie and Uncle Silas instead of staying down in Madison with her parents.

She sent Pearl a sly look. "And could there possibly be somebody else down in Madison you'd like to see besides Jericho and Tunia?" Since her last trip to Madison, Pearl hadn't stopped talking about Adam Chapman. The son of Jericho and Tunia's best friends, Andrew and Patsey Chapman, Adam seemed to have his sights set on a ministry in the African Methodist Episcopal Church.

"Maybe." The apples of Pearl's brown cheeks glowed with a faint rosy hue. "Got another letter from Adam jist yesterday. He's been studyin' hard for the pulpit."

Charity was glad she had taught Pearl to read, write, and cipher when they were young, despite the fact that it was against the law. The two had simply made a game of the secrecy.

"He's gonna be a right-fine preacher in the AME church one day." Pearl's chin lifted as she spoke of her friend's ambitions.

Charity wet a scrap of clean cotton material in the hot water and ran it over her face, neck, and bare arms. "And everyone knows," she said, forcing a serious tone to her voice as she finished dressing, "a preacher needs a wife."

"I got my eyes on that purty man, that's for sure." Pearl pulled a velvet-upholstered stool closer to the dresser and picked up Charity's hairbrush. "Now set yerself down and let me fix yer hair."

Smiling, Charity obeyed, allowing Pearl to brush her hair, then twist it into a knot, which she secured to the back of Charity's head with several pins. Although Charity had repeatedly offered to do her own hair, Pearl insisted on continuing the morning tradition they'd started as young girls in Georgia. It was during these times they had opportunities to share thoughts, giggle, and generally chat.

"High time you found a man o' yer own," Pearl said as she stuck the last couple of pins into Charity's hair.

Charity's shoulders rose and fell with her sigh. "I had a man, Pearl. He died with Asa at the Battle of Peachtree Creek."

Pearl rested her hands gently on Charity's shoulders. "Been more'n two years since Granger Hardwick done went to his reward." Her voice softened with her caring tone but held no hint of pity. "Memories ain't gonna keep you warm at night or give you babies to rock, neither."

After Granger's death, Charity had abandoned all serious thought of marriage. No one since had caused her heart to skip.

Not until Daniel Morgan appeared at the mill two weeks ago.

Pearl rounded the stool to face Charity. With her arms akimbo and fists planted firmly on her hips, she fixed Charity with a stern stare. "If I was you, I'd be schemin' on snarin' that nice-lookin' Mr. Morgan."

Heat leapt to Charity's face. "Well, you're not me. For your information, I'm plenty warm at night, I am definitely *not* lookin' for a husband, and I wouldn't know what to do with a baby if I had one. And as far as Mr. Morgan goes, I'm sure he has no interest in me and I certainly have no interest—"

Pearl gave a little gasp and shook her finger in Charity's face. "Don't you dare start yer day with a fib, Miss Charity. Hard tellin' what might happen if you was to go off to that mill 'neath the Good Lord's frown."

Rising, Charity threw back her head and laughed. When would she ever learn she could more easily fool herself than Pearl? "Have it your way, Pearl. I will admit the man is passably decent looking. But it doesn't change the fact that he's a Yankee. And if I ever do marry, it will certainly *not* be to a Yankee!"

Charity headed for the door. Aunt Jennie would be cross if she was tardy for breakfast and made Uncle Silas late to the mill.

Pearl touched her arm, halting her. "Come down to Madison with me, Miss Charity. I'd really like for you to meet Adam. And 'sides, without you along, that train ride's gonna be pure tedious."

The girl's dark eyes shone with the familiar pleading look Charity had found irresistible since they were children. "Mammy and Pappy'd like it if you come, too. Adam says they been pinin' they ain't seen you for the longest time."

Guilt pinched Charity's heart as she thought of her parents' former slaves. Aside from her deep affection for the couple, she knew that she owed both her virtue and her life to the Emanuels. When General Sherman ordered Atlanta's people to evacuate then burned the city along with outlying homes like hers, only God's grace and Jericho and Tunia's protection had brought her safely past the Union army and on to Indiana.

Charity gave her friend a fond smile. "I do miss them desperately and would love to see them. If Uncle Silas can do without me at the mill for a few days, I surely would like to accompany you."

Later that morning as she rode beside her uncle in the buggy, Charity broached the subject of joining Pearl on her trip to Madison. She was surprised at how quickly Uncle Silas agreed. "I've already bought your train ticket," he told her with a wink and a grin, adding that he'd decided to close the mill for a few days prior to the corn harvest.

"When the corn comes in," he said, lifting his hat to run thick fingers through his thinning gray hair, "we shall scarcely have time to take a breath." Giving the horse a cluck of encouragement as he guided it down the dirt path to the mill, he shot her a sideways smile. "We'd best all rest up in preparation."

Charity nodded, remembering last year's harvest. For weeks on end, the extra work required them to arrive at the mill before daylight and stay until after dusk. So when Joe Simms quit his job as mill foreman and moved to Versailles at the beginning of August, her uncle had been desperate to find a replacement.

Thoughts of the man who had taken Simms' place sent tingles dancing over Charity's skin. She hadn't spoken at length to Daniel since she'd corrected his mathematical mistake last week. To her shame, she'd considered leaving it alone for Uncle Silas to discover. But remembering the admonition from the scriptures, *"Therefore to him that knoweth to do good, and doeth it not, to him it is sin,"* she knew she had to fix it.

Inside the mill, Uncle Silas joined Daniel and Charlie, who'd already begun preparing the machinery for sawing a load of lumber.

At her desk, Charity went about organizing her morning's work. So when a scuffing sound brought her face up, she was surprised to find Daniel standing before her.

His gaze skittered around the small area but seemed unable to meet her eyes. "I just wanted to thank you for what you did for me last week—with Ed Cochrane's bill." He rubbed his forehead—a nervous habit that had become as familiar to Charity as his limp.

Trying to keep her voice indifferent, she shrugged and turned her attention to the desktop, needlessly rearranging stacks of papers. "If you are referrin' to the adjustment I made to Mr. Cochrane's bill, checkin' for such mathematical. . . irregularities is just part of my job." It wouldn't do for him to think she'd done him a special favor.

She watched his Adam's apple move as he swallowed—hard. His dark eyes glistened while several emotions flitted in turn over his features. At last, his tender gaze settled on her face and melted into her eyes, snatching away her breath. "You are a mighty fine woman, Miss Charity Langdon."

With her heart pounding in her ears, Charity's gaze dropped to the desktop. She could think of no intelligent response, which was just as well since she seemed to have lost the ability to speak. This man was indeed too troublesome by half! At least next week she would have a few days respite from his disquieting presence.

"I was happy to learn from Silas that you will be joining Pearl on a trip to Madison next week." His statement yanked her attention back to his face.

Confused, Charity stared at the smile crawling across his lips. "I cannot see how my travelin' plans could be of any concern to you."

A red stain spread from his neck to his face. "I'd assumed your uncle told you. Knowing I was also planning a trip to Madison next week to celebrate my sister's birthday, your uncle purchased three corresponding tickets and asked that I escort you and Pearl." His smile widened. "The three of us will be sharing a train car, it seems."

Charity gaped at him. "I see," she managed to mumble. Irritation squiggled through her as she wondered if Pearl had known of the arrangement when she'd invited Charity to join her.

She stared at the retreating figure of Daniel Morgan's broad back. Watching his halting gait carry him away from her desk, she knew there'd be no peace for her troubled heart.

four

Brightly whistling "Skip to My Lou," Daniel pulled the horse and wagon to a stop on Perry Street in front of Silas Gant's three-story brick home. He knew it was ridiculous to be so happy. The look of dismay on Charity Langdon's face when she'd learned he would be sharing a train car with her and Pearl had been plain. She clearly held him in disdain.

Yet he couldn't stop his heart from dancing as he jumped to the ground. Even the familiar stabbing pain in his leg caused by the jarring motion was eased by the thought of enjoying Charity's company for the twenty-five mile trip to Madison.

The wrought-iron gate gave a little squeak when he pushed it open. He crossed the neat little yard and stepped up to the porch, trying to ignore his pounding heart.

Pearl Emanuel answered his two quick raps on the door, a smile flashing from beneath the yellow calico bonnet framing her dark face. "We're all ready," she said, as he relieved her of two bulging carpet bags.

Charity, who'd joined Pearl in the hallway, greeted him with a silent nod and a stilted smile. She pushed a sizeable portmanteau toward the open front door while at the same time clutching a little carpet bag. Wearing a green dress and a becoming straw bonnet decorated with pink paper flowers, she reminded Daniel of a rose.

Not wanting her to find him staring, he turned his attention to depositing the luggage in the wagon. When he returned to the porch for Charity's carpet bag, Mrs. Gant bustled breathlessly into the front hallway waving a brown paper package tied with a gold cord.

"Charity," she said, the word puffing from her lips, "please deliver this small token of my regard to Miss Morgan in com-memoration of her birthday."

A look of dismay flashed briefly across Charity's face. It fled quickly and she turned a weak smile toward her aunt. "Of course, Aunt Jennie," she mumbled.

Daniel couldn't guess why Charity might find the thought of delivering a gift to Lucy disquieting. But she clearly did not relish the errand. Charity had never struck him as particularly shy, but he did remember Silas mentioning that Mrs. Gant felt their niece should socialize more. Perhaps, like Daniel, Charity had simply allowed her social graces to grow rusty during the war.

Daniel smiled at Mrs. Gant and reached for the package. "A gift is entirely unnecessary, ma'am. But I would be happy to deliver your kind offering to my sister and relieve Miss Langdon of the chore."

Mrs. Gant shook her head as she opened Charity's carpet bag, tucked in the box, then closed the bag again. "No, no. As it is from the three of us—Silas, Charity, and me—I think it only proper that Charity deliver it personally. I will have it no other way." The solidity of her tone coupled with her uptilted chin suggested the futility of further argument.

Charity turned a genuine smile to Daniel. "Thank you for your offer, Mr. Morgan. But I look forward to meetin' your sister and personally wishin' her a happy birthday." Whatever concerns had sparked her earlier look of apprehension, she'd obviously set them aside and put both her aunt's and Lucy's feelings ahead of her own.

Daniel's heart clenched at the thought as he took the carpet bag from Charity's hands and deposited it in the back of the wagon. These glimpses of her inherent goodness—sweetness— left him frustrated. How he longed to discover what key might open her heart, allowing him to share in the wonderful treasures he sensed lay buried beneath the debris of bitterness and distrust left by the war.

He helped Pearl up to the back seat of the wagon then turned to do the same for Charity. Perhaps if Charity and Lucy met, it could help in his efforts to win Charity's favor. He could think of no abler ambassador of goodwill on his behalf than his bubbly, sweet-natured sister. The thought buoyed his spirit.

An almost intoxicating whiff of rosewater tickled his nostrils, and his hands relinquished Charity's trim waist with regret. His heart ached. Would performing such courteous acts for her be the closest Daniel ever came to holding Charity Langdon in his arms?

Daniel climbed to the front seat of the wagon where Silas joined him and drove them the two and a half blocks to the Vernon railroad station.

The four-story hip-roofed brick station house jutted up against a hill of earth and stone nearly half the building's height. Three distant blasts of a train whistle announced that a locomotive would soon roll into view on tracks that ran along the top of the hill.

Charity, Pearl, and Daniel said their farewells to Silas on the station's long covered porch as the train rumbled to a hissing stop above them. Daniel paid two young boys to transport their luggage up to the baggage car as a porter's full-throated "Aaaall abooooard!" wafted down from the tracks above.

Through a rolling cloud of acrid coal smoke, Daniel followed Charity and Pearl up the dozen or so wooden steps to the waiting train. He wished he could sit next to Charity for the hour excursion but knew Pearl would be sharing the bench seat with her.

They made their way down the car's narrow aisle where the odors of stale cigar smoke and cramped humanity clung to the air. When Charity and Pearl were seated, Daniel slipped into the seat directly behind theirs.

A feeling of lighthearted anticipation filled Daniel as they chugged away from Vernon. As much as he'd needed to distance himself from his family's smothering care, he *had* missed them, especially Lucy. He was also eager to meet her fiancé. He'd been only mildly surprised to learn from her recent letter of her whirlwind romance with Pa's new apprentice.

He grinned. There was nothing remotely shilly-shallying about his little sister. When she made up her mind about something, it was full steam ahead.

Charity's mood showed marked improvement as well. She giggled and chatted gaily with Pearl as the train clacked and rocked over the tracks through open fields and shady glades. Daniel's heart thumped harder each time Charity cast a smile over her shoulder at him, inquiring about creek names and local landmarks. Perhaps his presence was not as odious to her as he'd feared.

When they passed over Graham Creek, Pearl gazed out the window beside her. "That creek reminds me of the time we caught yer brother, Asa, playin' hooky from school in the creek behind the cotton mill," she said with a laugh.

Charity's straw bonnet bobbed with her nod and the soft pink curve of her profiled cheek lifted in a grin. "We made him do all our chores for two solid weeks in exchange for our promise not to tell Mamma and Papa."

Pearl chuckled. "Pappy couldn't 'magine what got into that boy to cause him to do such a power o' work."

Charity's giggle joined Pearl's. "And then when Mamma found out from the schoolmaster that Asa had been taking off from school, she made him do another two weeks of extra chores."

Their laughter trailed off, leaving a somber silence.

"I miss Asa." The sadness in Charity's quiet admission stung Daniel's heart.

Daniel's smile fell. A sudden urge to offer Charity a word of sympathy struck, but his better judgment counseled him to stay silent. According to Silas, Charity's brother died serving under the Confederate flag. He surmised any offer of condolence from a former captain in the Union army would not be well received.

"I miss him, too," Pearl said softly, making Daniel glad Charity had such a close, dear friend with whom to share her tears as well as her laughter.

At last, the train finally slowed and they pulled into the long, enclosed train shed depot just north of Madison's Ohio Street. A warmth spread over Daniel as the building's familiar shadows wrapped around him like a comforting embrace. It was good to be home.

As they disembarked, he scanned the crowd milling about the dimly lit shed for his family. Almost at once, he and Lucy spied one another and, with a little shriek, she bounded toward him, beaming. Daniel caught his sister in a hug, lifting her off the depot floor. A little more than five years his junior, his baby sister would always occupy a special corner of his heart.

"How mean of you to stay away for so long, big brother. You know how I miss you." Lucy reached up to continue hugging his neck after he'd set her down.

"Hmm," he teased as he disentangled himself from his irrepressible sibling. "Now that you have a new man in your life, I doubt you've given me a moment's thought."

Lucy pinked prettily. "I can imagine your surprise at learning your spinster sister is finally getting married." Her bright blue eyes, so like their mother's, sparkled. "I can scarcely wait for you to meet Travis! You just missed him, leaving when you did for Vernon. He came the next week to apprentice under Papa. You two will get on famously, I just know it!" His sister linked her arm with his. "Papa and Travis are out calling on patients in Papa's buggy, so I brought the phaeton."

Suddenly remembering Charity and Pearl, Daniel resisted his sister's tugs and glanced over at the two women scanning the crowded depot, searching, he assumed, for Pearl's parents.

Heat marched up his neck. He would need to polish his rusty social skills so as not to embarrass his sister and mother when they dined tonight with Lucy's new beau.

He guided his sister to Charity and Pearl. "Lucy, I'd like for you to meet Miss Charity Langdon, my employer's niece, and her friend, Pearl Emanuel. They've come to Madison to visit Pearl's parents at Georgetown."

As the young women exchanged greetings, a middle-aged black man stepped toward them, dragging a battered felt hat off his graying head. Daniel recalled having seen him in the company of Andrew Chapman and surmised it must be Jericho Emanuel.

The man gave Pearl a warm hug. Then with a polite nod to the group, he mumbled something about fetching the luggage and headed toward the baggage car.

When Charity and Pearl turned back to Lucy and Daniel, Lucy's face lit with a look of revelation and she smiled at Pearl. "Oh, you are the young lady Adam Chapman is sweet on."

A sheepish grin stretched Pearl's lips and she cast a glance downward. "Reckon that road runs both ways, Miss Morgan. Jist glad he says so, though."

Then Lucy's look swung between Charity and Daniel. A mischievous glint in her eye sent warning ripples through Daniel. He held his breath, unsure what to expect from his outspoken sibling as Lucy settled her gaze on Charity.

"I hope we have an opportunity to visit during your time in Madison, Miss Langdon. I can see that Daniel's description of your beauty and grace was not in the least overstated."

Heat shot up Daniel's neck. He would tweak Lucy's nose for that comment on their way home.

A rosy hue suffused Charity's face, and then she gave a little gasp. "Oh, Miss, Morgan, I almost forgot. My aunt Jennie sent you a birthday gift." She cast a helpless look down the length of the train in the direction Pearl's father had gone. "But I'm afraid it is packed away in my luggage. Perhaps I can find Jericho—"

"Don't trouble yourself." Lucy shook her head. "I plan to open my gifts this evening at supper and would be most honored if you would attend and bring the gift with you."

Daniel's heart thumped quicker. He'd never imagined Lucy

would invite Charity to supper, but he doubted she would accept.

"Miss Langdon'd be right pleased to join you, ain't that right, Charity?" Pearl turned to Charity, across whose deepening pink face flashed a look of alarm.

"I. . . ." Charity shot Daniel a beseeching look, but he had no interest in assisting her in contriving a reason not to dine with him this evening. Her smile slowly widened as her gaze slid back to Lucy. "Thank you, Miss Morgan. I would be honored to attend."

Lucy clapped her hands, audibly expressing the glee silently bubbling up inside Daniel. "We will dine at six, so Daniel will pick you up at five thirty."

five

Daniel's heart quickened, keeping pace with the trotting hooves of the sleek black gelding bearing him and the open phaeton down Mulberry Street toward Georgetown. In a few moments he would see Charity. This was a pleasure he hadn't expected to enjoy again until three days hence, when he would accompany her and Pearl on the train ride back to Vernon. Although he had soundly chided an unrepentant Lucy for embarrassing him in Charity's presence this morning, he silently thanked his sister for this opportunity to spend some time alone with Charity.

Daniel pulled up in front of the neat, little, whitewashed shotgun house that belonged to Jericho and Tunia Emanuel.

The waning sun washed the late afternoon in a golden hue as he climbed down from the carriage and made his way up the porch steps. He hoped that despite her initial reluctant demeanor, Charity would enjoy Lucy's birthday dinner this evening. Indeed, the lovely, warm September afternoon gave him courage to believe she might actually enjoy his company as well as the carriage ride to his parents' home.

Jericho answered his quick raps on the door, and Daniel noticed the man was dressed in his Sunday best. "Miss Langdon'll be along directly, Mr. Morgan. We're fixin' to head down to the AME Church for a hymn-sing this evenin'."

Daniel nodded. His Uncle Jacob, who ministered at the church on Broadway Street, had mentioned that Andrew and Patsey Chapman's son, Adam, was studying for the ministry. He was about to comment on his uncle's joy in learning of Adam's choice of vocation when he glanced over Jericho's shoulder and saw Charity clutching Mrs. Gant's brown paper package.

Daniel felt as if he'd been punched hard in the midsection. Even in the common day dresses she wore to the mill, Charity Langdon was beguiling. He'd thought her enchanting when he saw her dressed in her Sunday finery the day he'd dined at the home of her aunt and uncle. But adorned in this pink silk evening frock, she was nothing short of stunning. Her golden hair, parted in the center, tumbled in long ringlets that brushed the white crocheted wrap covering her bare shoulders.

They made their parting salutations to the Emanuels, and Charity tucked her arm around Daniel's, sending a thrill through him. He hated that his game leg required him to grasp the railing to steady himself as they descended the porch steps. But even more painful was Charity's thick Southern accent that reminded him of why he limped.

"I suppose it was a good thing, after all, that my aunt insisted I bring an evenin' gown," she told him as he helped her into the carriage. "I hadn't imagined I would need one, but Aunt Jennie would not allow me to leave Vernon without a change of formal attire."

Daniel had never before heard Charity prattle on, especially about fripperies like women's fashions. He sensed she was nervous but couldn't discern if it was his company or simply the thought of dining with strangers that caused her unease.

"Thank you for attending Lucy's birthday dinner this evening," he said as he guided the horse onto Mulberry Street. "She and Mother are looking forward to your company. Normally, we would have a house full of women. Aside from my Aunt Rosaleen, I have four female cousins who usually attend these affairs. But my Aunt Rosaleen is tending my twin cousins, Rory and John, who are down with bad colds; my cousins, Lydia and Rose, have gone to visit their sister, Abigail, who attends a young women's academy in Cincinnati; and Lilly, my cousin Ruben's wife, is. . .in confinement and not socializing." Daniel's face warmed and he wished in his nervous blathering he hadn't mentioned his cousin who was awaiting the birth of her fifth child.

Charity fussed with the hem of her wrap, but he sensed her nervousness had nothing to do with his indiscretion. "It must be wonderful to have such a large family. You and your sister seem especially close."

The haunting, sad quality that tinged her words made him ashamed. He should have remembered she was an orphan before gushing about his large, extended family.

"Yes, despite our age difference, Lucy and I have always been close." The memory of Lucy nursing him back to health after he returned from the war—refusing to leave his bedside for days on end—flooded his mind. He couldn't help thinking of Charity's lost brother and broached the subject he'd shied away from earlier that day on the train. "Were you and your brother close?"

His heart shuddered when she became quiet.

When she spoke, her voice was so soft he had to strain to hear. "Yes, we were."

"I'm sorry. Many good men were lost." He wished he had obeyed his earlier inclination and not asked. They spent the remainder of the trip down Main-Cross Street to his parents' home in silence.

Later in the family parlor, Daniel was happy to see Charity's mood brighten beneath his mother's gentle graces and his sister's friendly exuberance. While Lucy opened her gifts, she and Charity giggled together like school girls.

"Aunt Jennie says a girl's hope chest is not complete without a fine set of doilies," Charity said, responding to Lucy's bemused look when she unwrapped the lacy white pieces of crochet work Mrs. Gant had sent.

Both girls glanced at Lucy's intended, who turned the color of a near-ripe strawberry.

Travis Ashby—whom Daniel liked immediately—was every- thing Lucy and his mother had advertised. During his service in the army, Daniel had learned to evaluate the character of a man very quickly. He soon found that a keen wit percolated beneath the young man's mop of curly, sand-colored hair. Travis's lively green eyes revealed a fun-loving nature Daniel could imagine was irresistible to his vivacious sister.

When she finished opening her gifts, Lucy led the way to the dining room, arm in arm with Charity. Seeing the two girls getting along so well ignited an inexplicable joy in Daniel.

After several minutes of Travis and Pa dominating the supper conversation with talk of medicine, Mother lifted an appealing look to Pa. "Please, Ephraim, no more talk of medicine. We must be boring poor Charity to death."

The corners of Pa's eyes wrinkled as he turned that familiar, adoring look on Mother's face.

How he loves her still. The thought struck Daniel with heartwarming poignancy as he watched his father's gaze caress his mother's features. Though the years had streaked her chestnut hair with silver and etched fine lines on her face, his mother remained a stunningly beautiful woman. Her vibrant blue eyes, so like Lucy's, shone as brilliantly as ever. Could he hope to be as lucky as his father and find a woman who so completely captured his own heart?

His gaze drifted with the muse to Charity's face. Wreathed in candle-glow, she looked absolutely celestial.

"Of course, my dear, you are right," Pa said, then turned toward Charity. "You have a lovely accent, Miss Langdon. From what part of the South do you hail?"

Charity blushed so prettily it made Daniel's heart ache. "Thank you for sayin' so, sir. I was born and raised in Peachtree, Georgia."

At her quiet declaration, a cold fist grabbed inside Daniel's chest. It had been just outside that town near Peachtree Creek that he, Tom, and Fred were captured by Confederate soldiers. Because of that capture, he spent six indescribably horrible months in Andersonville prisoner-of-war camp where his two friends and subordinates died.

Daniel noticed that the others around the table had grown quiet. Surely his family had guessed the ugly memories the mention of Peachtree, Georgia had evoked for him.

Blessedly, Travis piped up between bites of roast pork, filling the awkward silence. "Are you planning to return to Georgia sometime in the future, Miss Langdon? I hear much is already being done toward the restoration of the South."

The wistful look glistening in Charity's eyes pricked Daniel's heart. He remembered how acutely he'd missed his own home during the war. From the scraps of information he'd gleaned from Silas Gant and Charlie Brewster, Charity's family's property had been burned by General Sherman's troops.

"Yes, Mr. Ashby, I dream of the day I might return and reclaim my family's land and rebuild my home and cotton mill that was burned. . .durin' the war." She glanced at Daniel. The soft lines of her jaw seemed to harden slightly, and he glimpsed a flash of anger in her blue eyes. "That is, if some Yankee carpetbagger hasn't claimed it for his own."

After another stretch of uncomfortable silence, Mother wisely steered the conversation to the safer topic of women's fashion. The others, including Charity, grasped the subject like a lifeline.

But Daniel sat in miserable silence, tormenting a cooling heap of mashed potatoes with his fork. If he'd ever entertained a glimmer of hope that he might nurture a closer friendship with Charity Langdon, she'd just killed it.

six

The tantalizing aromas of grits, coffee, and sausage coaxed Charity awake, dispelling the fog of sleep shrouding her consciousness. She squinted against the sunlight streaming through the long, narrow window of the sparse little bedroom she shared with Pearl. But when she turned to wake Pearl, she found the other side of the bed empty, the covers rumpled.

Scooting her legs over the side of the mattress, she lazily stretched and yawned. Her bare feet pressed against the nubby warmth of the rag rug that covered white-painted floorboards beside the bed.

She dressed quickly. Perhaps Pearl had gotten up early to help Tunia with breakfast. Tomorrow they would be traveling back to Vernon. Most likely, Pearl just wanted to get an early start on their last day here.

Pearl had spent much of the past two days visiting Adam and his family. Last night she expressed regret for having left Charity alone at the house so much and had promised that today they would go shopping together. The evening Charity visited the Morgans had been her only time away from Georgetown since arriving in Madison, so today's outing would be a refreshing diversion.

Thoughts of Lucy Morgan's birthday dinner caused Charity's skin to tingle and her face to warm. She remembered how her heart had skipped a beat when she first caught sight of Daniel waiting to escort her to his parents' home. Tall and handsome in his dress clothes, he had stirred even more deeply the disquieting feelings he'd evoked in her since first appearing at her uncle's mill.

The memory of his strong hands on her waist as he helped

her from the carriage sent a renewed thrill through her. She tried to remember if she'd ever thought Granger so handsome or if his mere presence had caused her heart to flutter as it had the other evening with Daniel Morgan.

Shame sizzled inside Charity as she headed toward the kitchen. How could she be so disloyal to the memory of the man she'd planned to wed? She must not forget that Daniel Morgan could very well have looked across the battlefield, fixed Asa or Granger in his rifle's sight, and pulled the trigger.

"Done thought you was fixin' to sleep the day away, chil'!" Tunia glanced up from stirring a pot of grits on the stove, an ivory smile flashing from her dark round face as Charity entered the kitchen.

"Where's Pearl?" Charity returned the smile as she sat in a caned chair at the little rectangular table. Surrendering to another yawn, she smoothed a wrinkle from the red and white gingham tablecloth.

Tunia placed a plate of grits and sausage in front of Charity. "Adam come by early. Said his mammy's feelin' poorly today an' ain't up to helpin' Miz Hale down at the parsonage. Said Patsey was frettin' 'bout the rev'rend's wife havin' to manage two sick young'uns upstairs an' a parlor full o' church women by herself this afternoon. So she had Adam fetch Pearl down there to help." Tunia bustled about the stove, clearing away the breakfast remnants. "Reckoned I'd go see 'bout Patsey d'rectly, then head down to Rev'rend Hale's parsonage and help Pearl."

Disappointment pushed a sigh from Charity's lips. She understood Pearl wanting to help Adam's mother, but the situation relegated Charity to spending another day on her own.

A knocking at the front door sent Tunia padding through the house.

At the sound of Daniel Morgan's voice, Charity dropped her spoon back into the mound of grits on her plate. They'd planned to leave for Vernon tomorrow. What was he doing here today?

She jumped from her chair and hurried to join Tunia in the front room.

Tunia invited Daniel into the house then excused herself, mumbling something about the grits on the stove as she headed back to the kitchen.

At the sight of Daniel, that now familiar fluttering commenced in Charity's chest. "Daniel,"—she wished her face didn't suddenly feel so warm—"I understood we were not to leave until tomorrow."

"I'm not here to take you home." His large hands fiddled with the brim of his hat. "Lucy has planned a picnic for today and would like it very much if you would agree to join her, Mr. Ashby, and myself on the outing." He gave her a shy grin. "Lucy's dead set on a picnic at Cedar Cliffs." He cocked his head to the left. "It's a place a few miles east of Madison that overlooks the river."

Charity's heart pounded quicker, stoking the flames in her cheeks. Obviously, Lucy and Travis required chaperones for propriety. Lucy must have decided making it a foursome was preferable to just having Daniel tag along with her and Travis.

Charity couldn't deny she liked Lucy very much. Daniel's sister was just her same age. Under other circumstances, she would relish a friendship with Lucy Morgan. But spending time with Lucy meant spending time with Daniel—something she'd hoped to avoid.

"If you would rather not, I'm sure Lucy will understand."

Charity studied Daniel's expression. Was that disappointment she saw in his eyes? And if so, was it disappointment for his sister or for himself?

Charity glanced back toward the kitchen. Since Jericho, Tunia, and Pearl would all be gone from the house, an afternoon picnic seemed preferable to spending the day alone. "Tell Lucy I thank her for the invitation and would love to attend."

A smile slowly traipsed across his handsome face, and his

dark eyes that had dulled came alive. "We shall come by and pick you up about noon then." He gave a quick bow, turned, and headed toward his wagon. Even with his limp, there seemed to be an extra spring to his step.

Charity stood in the open doorway watching until Daniel's wagon disappeared around the corner. She turned and headed to the kitchen, wishing she weren't so eager for twelve o'clock to come.

❧

Four hours later, as she bounced beside Daniel on the buggy's front seat with Lucy and Travis seated behind them, Charity still questioned the wisdom of accepting the picnic invitation.

For the past two years, she'd endured the company of Yankees simply because she'd had no other choice. Though cordial to her Vernon neighbors, she'd nurtured few close friendships there, especially among people of her own age.

Lucy Morgan's friendly effervescence had revived memories of lighthearted friendships Charity had shared with other girls her age in Georgia before the war. Hadn't Charity prayed for God to help her forgive the trespasses committed against her by the Yankees? Perhaps a promising friendship with Lucy Morgan was part of God's answer.

Daniel turned the buggy onto a winding, wooded road that abruptly rose to a steep incline, and angled a grin toward Charity. "Better hang on tight." His handsome profile made her heart skip, and she had to remind herself that she'd agreed to join this picnic as a favor to Lucy, not so she could spend an afternoon with Daniel.

At last, they emerged from a grove of evergreens into an open, grassy expanse that overlooked the Ohio River, and Daniel pulled the buggy to a stop.

The pleasant smell of cedar scented the gentle breeze as Charity gazed down upon the river. The sight took her breath away. She'd seen the river up close several times. And two years ago, she and the Emanuels had crossed it as they neared the end of their perilous journey from Georgia. But from this height, the view of the river was nothing less than stunning. The wide, shimmering waterway was visible for miles, bending gently through woods tinged with the first golden touches of autumn's color.

After the men helped Charity and Lucy to the ground, Lucy gave Charity a hug. "Isn't this just the most delightful spot? I'm so glad you were able to join us, Charity." Bouncing with obvious excitement in her yellow linen-lawn frock, Lucy looked like an inverted buttercup in a stiff breeze.

"Thank you for invitin' me." The words left Charity's lips honestly and easily as she and Lucy each picked up one of the two quilts Lucy had brought and tucked it under an arm.

Lucy linked her free arm with Charity's. "Come. Let's find a good picnic spot while Daniel and Travis fetch the baskets."

Deciding on an area in the shade of a large cedar tree several yards from the buggy, Charity and Lucy worked together spreading the faded, patchwork quilts over the grass. At last they seated themselves on the pallets, adjusting their voluminous skirts around them with care.

"Perhaps we should have chosen a spot closer to the buggy," Lucy said quietly, her tone edged with regret.

Charity stopped smoothing wrinkles from her green cotton skirt and followed Lucy's gaze. Daniel and Travis, with picnic baskets in hand, had just started in their direction.

A pained expression pinched Lucy's features as she watched her brother's halting gait. "He was always so big and strong, I sometimes forget."

"Was it a bullet wound?" Charity asked the question she'd wondered about since Daniel first limped into her uncle's mill.

"No. His left leg was broken. . .during the war," Lucy offered simply, becoming suddenly reticent.

Charity sensed Daniel's sister was holding something back, but good etiquette dictated she should not pry further.

The men arrived, bringing with them the wonderful aroma

of fried chicken, and the conversation quickly turned to the picnic fare. Daniel and Travis sat cross-legged on the quilts, and Charity noted with interest that Lucy asked Travis, not Daniel, to offer grace before the meal.

Uncle Silas had mentioned that Daniel declined several invitations to worship with them at the little church on the hill overlooking Vernon. Yet his family seemed extremely devout. According to Tunia, Daniel and Lucy's uncle had long ministered at one of Madison's churches. Had Daniel rejected his faith? The thought made her sad. But when she sneaked a peek during the prayer, he had his head bent, his dark hair falling across his broad forehead.

Daniel Morgan was a puzzle, the pieces of which Charity told herself she had no interest in assembling. Yet she found herself eagerly listening as Lucy divulged incidents from his childhood.

"Daniel," Lucy said, pointing a chicken leg at her brother, "tell us about the time you saved Aunt Rosaleen when you were six."

Daniel squirmed and his face flushed. "I didn't save Aunt Rosaleen, Lucy. Uncle Jacob saved Aunt Rosaleen. And what would you know about it? You were just a baby." He shoved a forkful of potato salad in his mouth as if to put an end to the subject.

But Lucy would not be daunted. "I know plenty, because Mother told me," she countered, munching on a pickle. "Of course you saved Aunt Rosaleen. You told Uncle Jacob you saw that awful gambler abduct her."

"After Uncle Jacob shook it out of me," Daniel admitted with a self-effacing chuckle, then lifted his tin cup to his lips and took a long drink of the sweet tea Charity had made.

"Now you tell an interesting story about Lucy, Daniel." Travis's green eyes danced with fun as he reached over to tweak a glossy brown curl peeking from beneath his sweetheart's yellow bonnet.

Daniel shook his head. "Huh-uh! I'm smarter than that." His face took on a look of mock sternness when he turned it to Travis. "And I'd advise you not to ask about such things or my sweet sister just might shear those curls from your head like she did our neighbor's spaniel when she was five."

The mischievous grin he slid in Charity's direction set her heart prancing. This was a side of Daniel Morgan Charity hadn't seen. One she found both fascinating and endearing. It made her want to learn even more about him. A troubling thought.

Lucy smacked Daniel's arm. "Oh, you are horrid!" She joined the laughter around the quilt.

The playful banter between Lucy, Travis, and Daniel made Charity's heart ache. She remembered how Asa and Granger delighted in teasing her unmercifully. How she wished her brother was here to tease her about past escapades. Oddly, Asa's face remained vivid in her mind, while Granger's had faded to a blurry smudge.

The gentle look Daniel gave her suggested he sensed her sadness. . .and the cause of it. Was he remembering her admission the other evening on their way to Lucy's birthday dinner that she missed her brother? "I'm afraid we may be boring Miss Langdon with our silly reminiscences."

The kindness in his soft voice made Charity blink back hot tears. Why did he have to be so handsome, so charming. . .and so kind?

Renewed anger shot through her, stiffening her wilting resolve. She wouldn't accept compassion from a man who may have put Asa and Granger in their graves. Ignoring the thudding of her renegade heart, she brushed crumbs from her lap and lifted what she hoped was a cool, unaffected smile to him.

"Not at all, Mr. Morgan. In fact, I was about to ask if you and your sister recalled the occasion when Jenny Lind sang here in Madison in '51. My Aunt Jennie still talks about how she and my Uncle Silas traveled here to listen to the Swedish Nightingale sing in one of the old pork houses."

Lucy enthusiastically latched onto the topic, admitting that even at the tender age of six, she'd been awestruck by the sweet, pure quality of the woman's voice. "And I am convinced that at twelve, Daniel was entirely smitten by her. Why, I wouldn't be surprised if he doesn't still have that playbill with her picture on it tucked away somewhere in his room." Lucy grinned at her brother, whose tanned cheeks turned slightly ruddy.

They spent the next half hour discussing Miss Lind and her repertoire while devouring their picnic lunch.

While Daniel polished off the last piece of apple pie, Lucy began packing the lunch remnants and utensils back into the picnic baskets.

Charity followed her lead. She couldn't remember the last time she'd felt so carefree. . .so young. She'd actually shared a picnic with three Yankees and enjoyed it. Perhaps God was finally healing her heart and filling it with true forgiveness.

"Here." Lucy handed Daniel and Travis each a pie tin full of chicken bones. "Make yourselves useful and dispose of these somewhere in that grove of cedars."

With a salute from Daniel and a wink from Travis, they headed off to do her bidding.

Charity began helping Lucy fold up the quilts. "He's very handsome," she said, noting how Lucy blushed at Travis's wink.

"I've always thought so." Lucy glanced at the two men now several yards away as Charity transferred one end of a half-folded quilt into Lucy's hands. "Even if he *is* my brother," she added with a little laugh.

Heat leapt to Charity's face. "I was speaking of Mr. Ashby," she blurted breathlessly. How embarrassing to have Lucy think she found Daniel attractive!

Lucy laughed. "It's all right if you think Daniel is good

looking. You'd have to be blind not to." She shot Charity a conspiratorial grin. "Oh, don't worry. I won't tell him. And yes,"—she gave a dreamy sigh—"Travis is so handsome he makes my eyes hurt."

What Lucy might tell her brother wasn't nearly as worrisome to Charity as her own feelings about Daniel. She wished her heart didn't race so when she was near him. And that his dark smoldering gaze and handsome smile didn't snatch the breath from her lungs. She gazed at his tall, muscular form, his head thrown back, sharing a laugh with Travis.

Suddenly, a series of frightful images replayed in her mind. The ugly laughter of another tall, dark-haired Yankee echoed in her head. Again, she felt the soldier's fingers biting into her arm. Her kicking, flailing futilely as he dragged her to the cotton shed. The sounds of her dress ripping and her breathless sobs. Then the crack of Jericho's rifle butt on the soldier's skull. Then the blessed relief of being freed from the man's weight and sucking in grateful gulps of air untainted by the soldier's hot, whiskey-soaked breath.

A cold shiver shuddered through her.

What did it matter if Daniel Morgan had the ability to make her heart dance? It was also true that his mere presence could revive hideous memories for her. Agreeing to join this picnic had been a mistake. In the future, she must stay away from Daniel. . . and his family.

seven

"Well, it's a fine pickle he's left us in, and no doubt about it!" Iris Pemberton paused in her indignation. With pudgy fingers, she lifted a china cup from the tray Charity held out to her and murmured cursory thanks.

Aunt Jennie shook her head and made tsking sounds as she leaned forward on the horsehair sofa to retrieve a cup of her own. "Why on earth would the schoolmaster leave without a word and the school term about to commence?"

Taking a seat beside her aunt, Charity pasted on a smile and groaned inwardly. Iris Pemberton's latest calamity seemed as punctual as her afternoon visits. Obliged to help entertain Iris, Charity wondered why she'd looked forward to the end of harvest.

Two weeks after she returned from Madison, the local farmers' corn harvest began arriving at the mill, and October had passed in a blur. Twelve hours a day, six days a week, the mill bought load after load of corn, ground it, and then shipped it to various buyers via the Jefferson, Madison, and Indianapolis Railroad.

Charity had been forced to work closely with Daniel as he provided her with information for bills of sales and lading. Though she'd begun each day resolving to steel her errant heart against his charms, it regularly disobeyed her. Daily, her thoughts and affections were drawn toward him as if they were blossoms and Daniel was the sun. But at night, his sweet smile that lingered on her brain like a gentle shadow metamorphosed into the sneer of the soldier who'd tried to ravage her.

"Well, he won her affections, it would seem."

Iris's statement yanked Charity back to Aunt Jennie's front

47

parlor with a gasp.

"My sentiments exactly, Miss Langdon!" Iris dropped her teacup to its saucer with a punctuating clink. "No one I'm aware of even knew the schoolmaster was keeping time with the young Widow Foster. But whatever possessed them to elope to Cincinnati is beyond my understanding."

"Surely there must be someone else in Vernon who could fill in as teacher—at least until a permanent replacement can be found." Aunt Jennie offered Mrs. Pemberton the hopeful thought along with the plate of iced tea cookies.

"You would think so." Iris daintily plucked a cookie from the plate. "But my poor Cletus has scoured the town and can find no one willing or able to step into the position." She paused to wash down a cookie with a sip of tea.

Heaving a sigh, she dabbed at her mouth with her linen napkin before dropping it back into her ample lap. "Cletus had so hoped to win reelection to the office of school board president. But with this embarrassment, that buffoon Atwell will most likely beat him out."

"Perhaps if we put our heads together and listed all the relatively clever, unmarried young women in Vernon, we could think of someone," Aunt Jennie suggested.

Desperate to escape the parlor before the discussion digressed into a gossip session, Charity hefted the china teapot from the mahogany table beside the sofa. "Oh, the pot is nearly empty," she said, rising. "If you ladies will excuse me, I'll go brew—"

Suddenly Aunt Jennie and Iris Pemberton both looked at Charity as if they had never seen her before, halting her words in mid-sentence.

Aunt Jennie's face bloomed with inspiration. "Iris," she addressed her friend while gazing directly at Charity, "now that the harvest is over, Silas only requires Charity's services in the office one or two mornings a week. Silas could easily bring home what little bookwork there is for her to do now."

Hope flickered anew in Iris Pemberton's despair-dulled eyes. "Why yes, Miss Langdon. Your aunt has on more than one occasion remarked upon how well-read you are. I understand you have an amazing grasp of mathematics, and you are a spin—" Iris's face flushed at her *faux pas*. Any woman who'd reached Charity's age of twenty-two and remained unmarried was considered a confirmed spinster.

"Me, a teacher?" Charity sank back to the sofa, her knees suddenly wobbly, and plunked the teapot down on the table. She had never entertained the idea of becoming a teacher.

"You do like children, don't you?" Encouragement laced Iris's voice.

Aunt Jennie rushed to answer for Charity. "Well, she doesn't *dislike* them, I'm sure."

"No, of course I don't dislike children. I just don't know. . . ." The notion seemed so foreign. Charity strove to let it sink in. When she first came to live with Uncle Silas and Aunt Jennie, her work at the mill had seemed a natural transference of her role at her family's cotton mill. But this. . .this was something she'd never considered.

She suddenly found herself engulfed in Iris Pemberton's smothering embrace. "Oh, you are a godsend, my dear. A true godsend!"

"Thank you, Mrs. Pemberton, but since Pearl decided to stay in Madison after our recent trip there, I'm sure Aunt Jennie will need my help around the house." Charity worked to extricate herself from Iris's lavender-scented grasp.

Aunt Jennie gave a dismissive wave of her hand. "Iris has given me the names of several women who might be interested in a domestic position. I'm sure we'll have someone to take Pearl's place in no time."

Any further thoughts Charity might have regarding her teaching at the common school seemed to have been rendered immaterial. While Iris Pemberton and Aunt Jennie chatted excitedly about the upcoming school year and how they'd saved it, Charity sat in stunned silence.

The thought struck her that this might be God's answer to her prayers. For weeks, she'd entreated the Lord to take away the uncomfortable feelings Daniel Morgan evoked within her. In her mind, she'd imagined Daniel moving back to Madison and taking a job nearer his family. But she would not question God. This was obviously, at least in part, a Divine solution to her troublesome problem.

So why didn't she feel happier about it?

∂a

On Monday morning two weeks later, she trudged up Perry Street at the crack of dawn, her arms full of books and her heart full of trepidation. The November wind sliced through her light wool shawl, making her wish she had opted for her heavier one. Before the children began arriving, she would need to start a fire in the stove.

But as she neared the school, she was surprised to see wisps of light gray smoke curling skyward from the building's chimney. Charity hastened her steps. How would she garner the students' respect if one of them had arrived ahead of her?

When she approached the schoolhouse door, she noticed the wagon and mule parked outside the building. Her heart quickened. It was the mule and wagon Uncle Silas had given Daniel to use.

She hurried up the steps and pulled the door open. The schoolroom's inviting warmth met her. The place smelled of chalk, coal oil, and burning maple wood. She also noticed that the floor had been swept clean—another job that should have been hers.

Daniel knelt, feeding kindling into the black potbellied stove in the center of the room. He pivoted a quarter turn and cast a smile at her over his shoulder. "Thought you might enjoy a warm room for your first day of school."

"Yes. . .thank you." Charity hurried to close the door and keep out the chill.

Daniel rose, and it pricked Charity's heart to see him have to grasp a nearby desk to stand. "Well, I suppose I'd better be getting on to the mill." He took a couple of halting steps to the wall and plucked his hat from one of the pegs.

When he turned back to her, the shy look in his dark eyes melted her insides. She'd thought by taking this job, she'd escape Daniel Morgan and the uncomfortable effect he had on her. She hoped he wouldn't make this a daily ritual.

Charity hung her shawl on one of the wall pegs and strove to compose herself. How handsome he looked, even in his work clothes and that rumpled brown corduroy jacket.

She pasted what she hoped was a cool, aloof smile on her face. "Thank you very much, Mr. Morgan. I appreciate you preparin' the room for my first day. But as those tasks are part of my job as teacher, I will perform them from now on."

A hurt look flashed across his face for an instant before his smile dispelled it. "I wish you a good day, Miss Langdon." He plopped his brown felt hat over his head and slipped out the door.

Trying to put Daniel Morgan out of her mind, Charity moved behind the large desk at the front of the schoolroom and sank to the seat of the sturdy, well-worn oak chair. Suddenly something red caught her eye, and she picked up a shiny Winesap apple from the desktop. The ache in her heart burrowed deeper. Ridding herself of this worrisome feeling might be more difficult than she'd thought.

Thankfully, the children soon began arriving. After the brief introductions, Charity's lessons, which she'd spent hours preparing, demanded her full attention.

Charity found the eight boys and eleven girls, ranging in ages from six to thirteen, curious, attentive, and eager to please her. She suspected they enjoyed a change from the previous schoolmaster.

Happily, none of her students proved unruly or disagreeable. But she found one little fellow especially endearing. With his earnest attitude, sharp mind, and a Georgian accent to match her own, seven-year-old Henry Porter quickly claimed a special place in Charity's heart.

At noon, Charity was surprised to see the boy remain at his desk rather than joining the other children in the schoolyard. A glance at the floor along the wall beneath the coat pegs told her all of the lunch buckets had been claimed.

"Henry, didn't you bring a lunch?" Charity walked to his desk where he sat marking on his slate with his chalk.

Henry shrugged his narrow shoulders. "I didn't wake up in time to fix anything."

Anger flared inside Charity. What kind of mother left her child to fix his own lunch? "Why didn't your mother fix you something?"

"Ma's dead," he said matter-of-factly. "And Pa was still asleep."

At his desk, she looked down at his slate expecting to see a childish drawing. Instead, she saw a division problem. "Henry, the division problems are for the fifth grade students, not the second grade."

He shrugged again. "I know, but I like trying to figure them out."

Charity's heart went out to this little motherless son of the South who shared her love of numbers. "Very good," she said, picking up his slate to examine his work. "But look, you must carry this number forward." She picked up his piece of chalk to make the correction. "But that is enough work for awhile." She put down the slate and chalk and took Henry's hand, urging him up. This child would not do without lunch if she had to forfeit her own. "Why don't you come and share my lunch with me. I know I've packed more than I can eat."

"Henry." The man's voice that accompanied a brief gust of cold air stopped Charity and Henry, turning them toward the doorway. "I brought your victuals." The scraggly bearded, thin-framed man stepped into the schoolroom and held out a battered dinner tin.

Charity noticed that Henry accepted the lunch bucket with muted enthusiasm. Not having a mother, he'd probably thought it would be fun to share his new teacher's lunch.

Turning his attention to Charity, the man dragged his hat off his head, revealing a shock of sandy-colored hair the same shade as Henry's. "Forgive me for intrudin' ma'am, but I didn't want the boy to do without." His silky Georgian drawl caressed Charity's ears with the sound of home.

"Not at all—Mr. Porter, I presume?"

He dipped a deep bow. "Sam Porter, if I might be so bold as to introduce myself." His green eyes sparked. "I do believe I detect the accent of a Southern lady."

"Charity Langdon," she said. "I was born and raised in Peachtree, Georgia."

Sam Porter's face lit. "Why yes. I know the place very well. Before the war, my family owned Willow Grove Plantation just north of Atlanta."

Charity gave a little gasp. She could hardly believe her ears. Her family had done considerable business with Willow Grove Plantation. "You're one of the Willow Grove Porters? My family owned the Peachtree Creek Cotton Mill. We milled your cotton!" Her words came out in an excited rush.

"My, my." He shook his head and chuckled. "Fancy us meetin' up North like this. I'm surprised we didn't become acquainted at one of my mother's famous soirees." His eyes twinkled. "For if I had met you, I surely would have remembered."

Charity's face warmed. Though she found his gallantry admirable, surely he knew such an invitation would likely not have been proffered to the daughter of a mill owner. "I'm afraid I was affianced by the age of seventeen and didn't attend many soirees, Mr. Porter." At least her answer was true.

"And your young man?" The cautious tone of his question suggested he knew the answer.

"He fell at Peachtree Creek." She found herself relishing the attention of this Southern gentleman.

Sam Porter nodded somberly. "Please accept my sincere condolences. The South lost many a good man."

"Did you serve then, Mr. Porter?" The conversation had whisked Charity back to the Georgia that used to be. She smoothed her hands down the folds of her skirt, almost imagining she was entertaining a gentleman caller back home in her mother's parlor.

He straightened, standing a little taller. "Why yes, ma'am. I'm proud to say I fought under General P.G.T. Beauregard until I took gravely ill and was returned to my home." The muscles along his jaw hardened. " 'Bout the time I got on my feet, that devil Sherman's minions swooped down on our fair state, and me and my family had to run for our lives."

Sam's eyes exhibited the same distant, empty look she'd seen in countless pairs of Southern eyes since the war's end. His voice lowered to barely above a whisper and his shoulders sagged. "It's all gone now—Willow Grove, all our slaves, and even my parents. All gone." He cocked his head to the left. "We took refuge a few miles south of here in Clark County, Indiana, with my late wife's elderly cousin." He shook his head sadly. "Now they're both gone, too."

Charity offered an understanding nod. She was not surprised to learn that like her, Sam and his family had fled north as General Sherman's army poured into the South.

Then he gave her the lopsided grin she'd seen replicated on Henry's little face. "This past summer, I got work as a night watchman for the Jefferson, Madison, and Indianapolis Railway. That's what brought us to Vernon."

Charity understood now why Henry's father had been asleep when Henry left for school. The war had displaced so many people from her native state. She wondered how many times a similar scenario had played out among her fellow Southerners. "At least the Lord has blessed you with a fine son." She smiled fondly at Henry, who opened the dinner pail, releasing the smell of bacon.

"Yes, I suppose He has." Sam Porter seemed eager to linger while Henry quietly ate his lunch at his desk. "I've been thinkin' I need to get Henry back to church. My Bess—God rest her soul—would want that." Sam's face brightened as with sudden inspiration. "What church do you attend, Miss Langdon—it is *Miss*, I presume?"

"Yes, it is." There seemed to be something almost too smooth about Sam Porter, but Charity found herself drawn to these fellow refugees from her home state. "I attend the little brick church just up the road here at the top of the hill. I would like to extend the hand of Christian fellowship and invite you and Henry to worship there with our congregation this Sunday."

Sam's gaze held Charity's for a long moment. "Why, thank you, Miss Langdon." He lifted her hand and brushed his lips gently across the back of it. "May I say it's been a true pleasure to make your acquaintance? I very much look forward to seein' you at church this Sunday." His lingering gaze left little doubt that he would like to become better acquainted with her.

He tousled his son's hair. "You be good for Miss Langdon now, you hear?" Though lightly said, Sam's parting admonition seemed lacking in warmth.

Munching his bacon sandwich, Henry nodded mutely.

When Sam had gone, Charity walked to her desk and sat in the oak chair. She gazed at the boy who'd remained curiously quiet during the entire conversation between her and his father, then picked up the apple from the desktop and took a bite. The fruit filled her mouth with sweetness and just enough tartness to tingle the inside of her jaw. Sam Porter, she reflected, was not a bad-looking man. And he had displayed the same impeccable manners she had observed in the most refined Southern gentlemen. So why wasn't she more excited by the fact that he had shown a decided interest in furthering their acquaintance?

She took another bite of the apple Daniel had left for her. Looking at the fruit in her hand, she knew the answer.

eight

"Just a couple of Rebs. They deserve each other!"

Daniel stood at the mill's window and mumbled the disparaging sentiment, which he immediately regretted. The words didn't relieve the pain in his heart. Nor did the sight below amend his opinion of the mill's new employee. He didn't like Sam Porter one little bit.

Scowling, he watched Porter drive one of the freight wagons into the mill yard with Charity at his side. Since the war, he'd seen many men like Porter—spoiled sons of Southern planters. Deprived of their lavish, indolent way of life, they'd found themselves with few skills and little ambition and ill-equipped to carve out a decent living.

It hadn't pleased Daniel to learn that it was Charity's urgings that prompted Silas Gant to hire the Southerner to haul grain to the train depot and lumber to paying customers. Ironically, it was Daniel who'd suggested they needed to hire an additional man in order to free him and Charlie Brewster from the time-consuming tasks. But when he learned that Porter had been sacked from his night watchman's job for the railroad, Daniel had questioned the wisdom of Gant's choice.

Also, Daniel had to admit that the man's thick Southern accent was an added daily irritant he could well do without. As he'd done with Charity, Daniel had fought the repugnant feelings Porter's accent evoked. The war was over. It was patently unfair to scorn people simply because of their speech. But unlike his reaction to Charity, Daniel had sensed an innate meanness in the man.

He'd witnessed no particular act that would deem Porter unfit to work at the mill. But he'd seen a series of troublesome incidents that he felt revealed a base, malicious nature in the man. To Daniel's mind, Porter was far too quick with the whip when driving the mules. On more than one occasion, he'd seen him kick the cats that prowled the mill. And yesterday, when Charlie Brewster smashed his thumb while tightening the tension on the idler pulley, Porter actually sneered.

Daniel jerked away from the window, his scowl deepening. Last week, he'd overheard Porter offering to squire Charity to Sunday services. A flash of jealousy shot through Daniel. He feared that since Porter was a Southerner, it might blind Charity to the man's true character.

The tight frown in Daniel's forehead relaxed only a bit when Charity entered the mill, a serene smile gracing her lovely lips. The expression on her face caused a painful stab in his chest. Was her happy mood the result of having been in Porter's company?

Even now in the midst of November's chill, her presence felt like a warm spring breeze against his heart. Since she'd begun teaching, he hadn't seen nearly as much of her. He found himself looking forward to these Saturday mornings when she came in to bring the mill's weekly paperwork up to date.

"Good morning, Daniel." Her smile widened to a bemused grin. "You look as if you had pickles for breakfast," she said with a chuckle. Her twinkling eyes set his heart frolicking like a colt in an April pasture.

"Sorry," he mumbled, "I suppose I just have things on my mind."

Why did she have to be so beautiful? He tried to think of something he might say to warn her about Porter. But however he might fashion such a warning, she was sure to dismiss it as nothing more than his bias against Southerners.

She brushed past him, leaving his heart aching and the scent of rosewater tickling his nostrils.

Later, as Daniel worked to grind a load of grain to be shipped to Indianapolis, he couldn't get Charity and Porter off his mind.

Several times he'd noticed Porter slip away to Charity's little office.

A scripture from Proverbs flashed into Daniel's mind. *"A sound heart is the life of the flesh: but envy the rottenness of the bones."*

It must be true. His heart felt anything but sound, and he ached all the way to his bones.

When Daniel went to close the sluiceway gate above the overshot wheel to stop the operation, he noticed Porter heading once again toward Charity's office. Irritation bristled through him. At least he had a reason to go chase Porter away from Charity. The ground corn needed to be bagged, loaded on the wagon, and taken to the depot before two o'clock.

What he saw when he reached the open doorway of Charity's little cubbyhole-sized office made his blood boil. Sam Porter was bent over Charity's hand, kissing it.

"Porter!" He barked the man's name, causing both Porter and Charity to jump. "The corn is ready to bag." He fixed the man with a glare. If Porter wanted to court Charity, he would need to do it away from the mill. That thought, however, offered Daniel's heart no ease.

An icy animosity glinted from Porter's eyes. "I'll be right there, *boss.*"

The emphasis the man put on the last word skated very close to insubordination, straining Daniel's temper to its limit.

Porter turned back to Charity, whose cheeks had turned a deep rose color. "I will see you Thursday then. Henry and I are both lookin' forward to it." With that, he turned and headed out of the office. When he passed Daniel, his knee bumped against Daniel's bad leg. Although he mumbled an apology, Daniel had the distinct feeling the man had done it on purpose.

When Sam had gone, Daniel ignored his better judgment and blurted out his thoughts. "Miss Langdon—Charity,"— since their time together in Madison, Daniel felt relatively comfortable calling her by her given name, hoping to encourage her to continue reciprocating in kind—"your personal relationship with Mr. Porter is none of my business, but—"

"Mr. Porter is the parent of one of my students. Nothin' more." Charity's face reddened. Her back stiffened, and her chin lifted a good inch.

Heat raced up Daniel's neck. "I never meant to suggest anything improper. . . ." What a mess he was making of things! If he'd set out to make her detest him, he couldn't be doing a better job.

Her features relaxed and her sweet smile returned, warming him all the way to the center of his heart. "I'm sure you didn't, Daniel. I cannot expect you to be familiar with Southern traditions of etiquette. I simply invited Mr. Porter and his son to Thanksgiving services at our church and dinner afterwards."

Charity's gaze dropped for an instant to her desktop before returning to his eyes. Was that a look of shyness that flitted over her face? More likely it was embarrassment that he'd caught Sam kissing her hand.

"We—that is, Uncle Silas, Aunt Jennie, and I—would like very much to extend the same invitation to you. Unless, of course, you have plans to travel to Madison to visit your family on Thursday."

Her obvious disconcertion sent ridiculous shivers running through him. He would like to think that her nervousness was caused by his nearness. But more likely it was because she found extending the Gants' invitation to him distasteful.

"No, I hadn't planned to go to Madison. A train trip doesn't seem worth it for one day. I reckoned to do with whatever repast Mrs. Kilgore offered at the boardinghouse."

"Then can we expect you for dinner Thursday after church?" Was he imagining the hopeful gleam in her eyes?

Daniel's first inclination was to decline the offer. But maybe better to accept the invitation and keep an eye on Porter than to lie on his bed in the boardinghouse and stew all day

Thursday. "I would be honored—and thankful," he said with a small laugh, hoping the reply didn't make him sound as much of a dunderhead to her ears as it did to his.

Daniel returned to work with a conflicted heart. The joy of knowing he would be spending Thanksgiving Day with Charity Langdon was dulled by the realization that they'd be sharing the day with Sam Porter.

nine

As their buggy crested the steep incline leading up to the church, Charity scanned the churchyard. She, Uncle Silas, and Aunt Jennie had made arrangements to meet Sam and Henry there before the Thanksgiving service. But Charity knew her sweeping gaze wasn't seeking out the Porters.

Last week, the look in Daniel's dark eyes when he agreed to come to Thanksgiving dinner had set her heart bouncing in her chest like an India rubber ball. But he'd made no promise to attend worship services.

Uncle Silas guided the matched pair of sorrels to the hitching post beside the church. Charity saw no sign of Daniel, and her heart sagged with her shoulders. Of course it was her Christian duty to hope others would worship in the Lord's house and to encourage them to do so at every opportunity. But she knew there was more to her disappointment at Daniel's absence. Somehow, despite her resistance and denials to the contrary, Daniel Morgan had become important to her.

When Uncle Silas lifted her from the buggy, the sight of Henry Porter's little smiling face buoyed her heart. Standing with his father near the church steps, he waved his hat to get her attention.

Sam Porter chastised his son's exuberance with a quick cuff to Henry's ear.

Charity gasped at the sight. Though sorely tempted to express her disapproval at the man's harsh action, she exercised restraint. Sam did lack the gentling presence of a wife to help raise his son.

Sam strode toward her, wearing a smile as wide as the one he had, a moment earlier, squelched from his son's face. "Miss

Langdon," he drawled out her name and dipped a deep bow. His too-tight, outdated gray wool coat stretched taut across his shoulders as he bent. The garment was clearly from his youth, before his shoulders had broadened.

Two weeks ago, when Henry had come to school in tears saying his father had lost his job with the railroad and that they might have to go to the poorhouse, Charity knew she at least had to try to help.

At first glance, it had seemed unfair to her that the railroad should sack Sam for only one instance of falling asleep while on the job. But last month, two brothers named Reno brazenly robbed a moving train a few miles east, near Seymour. So considering the extraordinary recent event, she better understood the railroad's heightened interest in security.

Unable to bear the thought of Henry suffering from his father's mistake, she'd convinced Uncle Silas to hire Sam as a teamster. The moment Sam began working at the mill, his attentions toward her intensified.

Pearl had told her some time ago it was high time she found a man. Sam was a fellow Georgian with the kind of Southern manners that made Charity feel at home. But despite her attempts to talk her heart into doing so, it refused to swoon for Sam Porter.

Henry tugged at her skirt, his hopeful face tilted up toward hers. "Will we have turkey for dinner, Miss Langdon?"

Charity laughed lightly. Although Sam had not managed to capture her heart, his son definitely had. She smoothed the boy's sand-colored hair away from his face. Today's Thanksgiving feast would be a rare treat for this motherless child. "Yes, Henry, we have a huge one baking in the oven right now," she said, taking his little hand in hers as he licked his lips in anticipation.

She was still smiling when Sam offered her his arm. Just as she tucked her free hand in the crook of his elbow, the clip-clop of hooves on gravel turned her toward the lane leading up to the church.

Daniel's gaze met hers, but no smile touched his lips. From atop his bay stallion, he gave her a stony look and a terse nod.

Her heart performed its now familiar little flip in response to Daniel's presence. A feeling akin to resentment squiggled through her. If not for its stubborn insistence on being shackled to that Yankee, her heart would be free to care for Sam.

Jerking her head around, she tipped her face up to Sam's and gave him a wide smile. Perhaps if she just put her mind to it, she could divert her affection to a man more suited to her—a man whose son she adored.

Throughout the service, Charity's attention continued to drift unbidden across the aisle. More often than not, her look was met by Daniel's dark, piercing gaze.

Following the sermon, Reverend Davenport entreated the congregation to stand and join in singing the hymn, "Come, Ye Thankful People, Come."

Charity glanced over at Daniel to see his scowl slide in turn from Sam's face to Henry's and then to hers. Aggravation prickled along her spine. Daniel's dislike of Sam had been obvious from the man's first day at the mill. To her understanding, Sam had never been late to work or missed getting a load of grain or lumber to its destination in a timely fashion. She surmised Daniel's disapproval of the man sprang from the fact that he was a Southerner. She could hardly blame Sam for responding negatively to Daniel.

Outside in the churchyard after the service, the two men regarded one another with an icy formality. Charity hoped their animosity toward one another wouldn't mar the day's enjoyments for Henry.

Several minutes later, the group arrived at the Gants' home. A cornucopia of savory and sweet smells greeted them as they all filed into the front parlor.

Henry licked his lips and his eyes grew large as he took in the elegant room. "It looks like a king's house," he said with a long, low whistle then looked up at his father. "Is this like the house you grew up in at Willow Grove?"

Sam frowned and thumped the back of his son's head soundly. "Mind your manners, boy!"

Charity had been about to follow Aunt Jennie into the kitchen to assist her and the hired girl Aunt Jennie had found to help with today's big meal, but seeing Henry's eyes well with tears, she stayed. "That must mean I'm a princess," she said, hoping to divert his attention from his father's chastisement.

"You look like one." He gave her a shy smile, and his little ears turned bright pink.

"I agree." Daniel's quiet voice drew Charity's attention across the room. His gaze caught hers in a tender grasp and she suspected her warm cheeks matched Henry's ears in color.

Glowering at Henry, Sam muttered something about children needing to be seen and not heard.

At his father's withering look, Henry took two quick steps backward. Before Charity could warn him, he knocked into the little mahogany table beside the sofa. It teetered, sending Charity's favorite picture of her mother crashing to the floor.

"Henry!" His son's name exploded from Sam's mouth, and his features turned nearly purple. He jerked Henry by the arm toward the picture on the floor. "You pick that up!"

Sam turned to Charity and cleared his throat. The embarrassment registering across his red face suggested he wished the floor would swallow him up. "I must apologize for the boy's clumsiness. Don't know what's got into him."

Henry seemed unable to move, a look of horror distorting his frozen face, and Charity's heart broke for him. "I'm sorry, Miss Langdon." The barely audible words shook from his tiny voice while tears slipped down his tortured face.

Ignoring Sam, Charity crouched and gave Henry a hug and wiped the tears from his cheeks. "Why, it's just a little ol' picture, Henry. Don't you give it another thought, you hear?"

Uncle Silas, looking uncomfortable, waved his hand to

dismiss the incident. "That's right, Porter," he told Sam. "No real harm done."

Turning her attention to her mother's picture, Charity saw that although the photograph itself seemed undamaged, the glass covering it had shattered, and a large chunk of the walnut frame's corner had chipped off. But determined not to let Henry see her dismay, she hurried to deposit the damaged picture in the little drawer at the front of the table.

"I never really liked that frame, anyway," she told Henry with an indifference she didn't entirely feel and shoved the drawer shut. As she started to rise, strong fingers gripped hers, helping her up. She thought Sam had stepped forward to assist her, but straightening, she met Daniel's gaze and her breath caught. The look in his dark eyes could only be described as admiration.

Once again, she wished Daniel Morgan's presence didn't always make her feel off-balance and breathless. To hide her disconcertion, she turned, took Henry's hand, and led him into the dining room.

Aunt Jennie and the hired girl were loading the long cherry table with a tantalizing array of delicious-smelling dishes. Charity hoped Henry would forget the accident and enjoy the meal. But even the huge, roasted turkey steaming from the center of the table and its tempting aroma did little to brighten his demeanor.

After Uncle Silas gave the blessing, the conversation among the adults turned to such topics as the price of grain and the weather.

Charity glanced across the table at Henry's long face. Her heart wept for him as she watched him poke unenthused at the sweet potatoes on his plate.

Sam, seated beside Henry, seemed oblivious to his son's suffering. Between bites of cornbread dressing, he regaled Aunt Jennie with anecdotes of sumptuous dinner parties given at the plantation home of his youth.

It bothered Charity that Sam paid no heed to Henry's

discomfort. But she knew a father couldn't be expected to take notice of a child's feelings like a mother would. She was again struck by the notion that the two desperately needed a woman's presence in their lives.

She prayed God might give her something to say that would lift Henry's spirits. But before she could think of something, Daniel—seated next to her—spoke up.

"You know, Henry," he said, causing the boy to raise his drooping chin, "when I was about your age and visiting a neighbor's home, I did something far worse than breaking a picture. And my offense was compounded by the fact that I did it on purpose."

Charity almost choked on her bite of mashed potatoes. Daniel's words seemed anything *but* an answer to her prayers. How callous of him to humiliate Henry further by bringing up the embarrassing incident! She shot him a sideways barbed look which, if he noticed, he chose to ignore.

But Henry gave no indication that the comment bothered him in the least. In fact, he looked surprised and pleased that an unfamiliar adult had addressed him at the table.

"Once when I accompanied my father to the home of Mr. Lanier, the richest man in town," Daniel went on, "I was fascinated by the crystal drops hanging from one of the table lamps in his front hall." Daniel paused to take a bite of turkey and wash it down with a swig of tea. "Well, sir, I noticed how the baubles made little rainbows on the wall, and I decided Mr. Lanier, being so rich, would never miss a couple. So when Pa wasn't looking, I stuffed two in my pocket."

The reactions to Daniel's confession were as varied as the diners around the table. Henry's mouth gaped, and Aunt Jennie gave a little gasp. Uncle Silas guffawed, while Sam became sullen.

Daniel grinned. "When Pa found out what I'd done, he marched me right back to Mr. Lanier's house. After I apologized and gave him back the glass baubles, I, at my father's urging, promised Mr. Lanier that I'd pull all the weeds from the acre of fencing around his considerable yard."

"Did you get a belt-tannin'?" Henry asked, his eyes growing wide.

Daniel shook his head. "No. Whenever I or my sister did something wrong, Pa wanted us to learn a real lesson from it. And he always said little was ever learned at the end of a belt." He finished the sentence with a pointed look at Sam, who responded with a sarcastic snort.

Remembering Sam's rough treatment of Henry, Charity pressed her napkin to her mouth, stifling a smile. She hoped Sam might take Daniel's father's opinion to heart.

"So what did you learn?" Henry asked around a bite of sweet potatoes, now fully engaged in both the meal and the story.

Daniel stabbed a piece of turkey, and his gaze slid from Henry's attentive face to Charity, setting her heart thumping. "I learned never again to take anything that wasn't mine, the Ten Commandments forward and backward, and that after pulling an acre of weeds, even lye soap won't get all the grass stains off your hands."

Everyone around the table laughed appreciatively except for Sam, who remained dour-faced.

Charity sent up a special prayer of thanksgiving that God had found a way to restore Henry's joy.

But no joy shone from Sam's face. Instead, he glowered at Daniel. For an instant, the two men's steely glares crossed like rapiers over the Thanksgiving table.

As much as she would like to deny it, for Charity, there was no question as to the hero of the silent duel. He had raven-black hair, hypnotically dark eyes, and no Southern accent.

ten

"Perhaps I should just go to church with Uncle Silas and Aunt Jennie as I always do." Pushing the lace curtain aside, Charity gazed out of her bedroom window on the courthouse square below, knowing full well she could not change her plans at this late hour. In doing so, she would disappoint little Henry and embarrass Aunt Jennie.

She felt as drab and cold as the winter scene outside her window. Since Thanksgiving, she'd made a concerted effort to deepen her relationship with Sam Porter. But as she waited for Sam and Henry's arrival, something closer to dread than joy filled her chest.

She'd told herself that God, in His infinite wisdom, had gifted her with the affections of a Southern gentleman— something rare this side of the Mason-Dixon Line. Obviously, Henry—whom she adored—needed a mother's gentle touch. And Sam needed a tempering influence in his life, especially in regard to his parenting of Henry. Since Sam and Henry had begun attending church, she'd made every effort to encourage them to continue the practice. So when Sam offered to escort her to church this morning, she'd agreed without hesitation.

Frowning, she allowed the curtain to fall across the window, obscuring the dismal view, and turned away, rubbing her arms. Regret ached in her bones like the early December chill. It all seemed so perfect. So why didn't it *feel* perfect?

Perhaps that was why she liked numbers. When it came to ciphering, there was no murkiness. Her father's old saying concerning arithmetic flashed to the front of her mind. *"Figures don't lie."* Through proper calculation, one came to the correct answer, and that was the end of it. Pure and simple.

Sadly, other facets of life lacked the clarity of mathematics.

The bedsprings creaked in gentle protest as she sank to the edge of her bed with a sigh. She glanced up at the ticking clock on the fireplace mantel, and a tiny stab of panic attacked her midsection. In less than fifteen minutes Sam would be pulling up in front of the house.

Slowly, she forced herself to her feet and lifted her dark woolen cloak from the foot of her bed. "Dear Lord, if Sam and Henry are to be my future, then why do I feel so miserable?"

The answer to her prayerful, mumbled plea came like a rasped whisper, echoing from somewhere deep in her tormented brain. . . .

Daniel.

An elusive ache she didn't want to investigate throbbed in her chest. She thought again about how he'd attempted to alleviate Henry's distress at breaking her mother's picture by recounting an embarrassing story from his own youth. That simple act of kindness toward the boy had touched her deeply.

Yesterday at the mill, she'd noticed the disapproving look on his face when she accepted Sam's invitation to church. Although reason argued she shouldn't care one whit about Daniel Morgan's opinions, the memory remained vexing. And neither the cheery fire crackling in the fireplace nor the weight of the wool cloak enveloping her could dispel the dampness from her spirit.

She lifted her mother's worn Bible from the table by the bed and pressed it to her bosom. "Lord, take this feeling from me. Clear the way so that I might grasp, unencumbered, the future You have planned for me."

The prayer had no sooner left her lips when the distant sound of metal-banded wagon wheels crunching on gravel jerked her up with a start. She glanced out of the window and down on Perry Street. Sam and Henry had arrived. Her heart, which should have perked with gladness, sagged with resignation. Expelling another deep sigh, she plodded out of her room and down the staircase.

Charity's discomfiture intensified over the course of the morning. The more time she spent in Sam's company, the less she enjoyed it.

The subject of Reverend Davenport's sermon was peace. When he read the scripture from Isaiah 32:17, the words smote Charity's conscience as if God had breathed them directly into her ear.

" 'And the work of righteousness shall be peace; and the effect of righteousness quietness and assurance for ever.'"

She glanced down at Henry seated next to her in the pew, and a deep sadness gripped her. Her spirit felt neither quiet nor assured. If the effect of righteousness was peace, then what she was doing must not be right. In all good conscience, she could not allow the boy to believe she would one day become his stepmother when she felt no true affection for his father. With this thought in mind, she resolved to rebuff any future attentions from Sam, including accepting his offers to squire her to church.

So the following Tuesday when the invitation to Lucy Morgan and Travis Ashby's engagement party arrived in the mail, Charity was torn. If she accepted, it would mean she'd most likely be traveling on the train to Madison with Daniel Morgan and spending a considerable amount of time next weekend with him and his family. A disconcerting thought. But at the same time, it would effectively distance her from Vernon—and Sam Porter.

Beyond that, she would get to see Pearl again. Although not entirely unexpected, Pearl's decision not to return to Vernon after their trip to Madison in September had come as a blow to Charity. Yet knowing Pearl and Adam Chapman were on the verge of becoming engaged and would probably soon marry, she fully understood her friend's desire to be closer to her loved ones. But with Pearl's departure, Charity had felt acutely the loss of daily talks with her childhood friend.

Wednesday afternoon when she closed the schoolhouse door for the day, she still struggled with her decision about Lucy's party. Heading to the street, she hugged to her chest the little leather satchel filled with papers she would be grading this evening. The December wind bit her cheeks and whipped at her cloak as she trudged toward the apex of Perry Street. A sense of loneliness dragged her spirit down with her shoulders.

Squinting, she lifted her face to the gray sky. Icy crystals, which were not quite sleet yet not quite snow, pelted her cheeks. Ahead on her left, the little church loomed. Its sturdy brick façade beckoned, promising a haven for both her body and her spirit. As she did every Wednesday afternoon, old Annie Martin would be tidying the sanctuary in preparation for next Sunday's services.

Charity glanced down the hill. Uncle Silas and Aunt Jennie's home sat across from the courthouse, no more than fifty yards ahead. The weather was not so inclement that she needed to take immediate shelter. But looking up at the church, she knew it was the thought of Annie Martin's company more than the shelter that drew her.

She longed for a female confidante. Although she knew her aunt cared for her, Charity had never been especially close to her mother's sister. Aunt Jennie's personality so differed from her own that they rarely shared intimate conversations.

She turned toward the church, climbed the four stone steps, and pulled open the heavy front door. Slipping quietly inside, she was met by the smell of linseed oil, old books, and wood smoke.

"*Faites attention!* Be careful, *ma chère.* I have just swept the floor." Annie Martin poked her head, covered by a black wool bonnet, above the tall back of the front pew. "I would like to keep the mud out until everyone tracks it in Sunday morning." The crevices at the corner of her light brown eyes etched deeper with her smile.

"I'll be careful, Annie." Charity grinned as she slipped into the back-most pew.

Annie's coarse, dark wool skirt swayed with her ambling gait as she made her way to the back of the church, glancing down each pew as she passed. Charity knew she was checking to see that each held its allotted number of hymnals. When she came to the pew where Charity sat, she scooted in beside her.

The old woman cocked her head and fixed Charity with a curious look. Wispy curls of silver hair that still showed traces of auburn peeked out from the bonnet framing her aged face.

"So, ma chère, are you here to talk to me or to God?"

Charity smiled. She always loved listening to the woman's accent, which she'd inherited from her French fur-trapper father. "Maybe both," Charity said with a sad smile. She began telling her about Daniel, Sam, and Henry Porter, and her quandary concerning whether or not to accept Lucy Morgan's invitation. "I've tried to care for Sam for Henry's sake, but—"

"But your heart bends toward Mr. Morgan instead." Annie's eyes, cinnamon-brown and flecked with amber, studied Charity's face.

Charity started to open her mouth to object to Annie's accurate deduction but shut it. There was no use in denying it. Annie Martin was far too astute. "Yes." The admission puffed out in a weary breath. It felt good to finally release the truth from its prison deep within her heart. Unwilling to meet Annie's gaze, she looked down at her hands clasped in her lap.

"And Mr. Morgan? He shows you no interest, ma chère?"

"Oh, no—I mean yes—yes, he does. In fact he. . ." Charity looked up, and heat leapt to her face at the knowing grin lifting the corners of Annie's mouth.

Annie took Charity's hands in her gnarled fingers. "Then why, ma chère? Why spurn the man your heart desires and try to force it toward one it rejects?"

Charity felt her jaw go slack at the absurdity of Annie's question. Surely Annie could guess the reason. "Because Daniel

Morgan is a Yankee," she blurted. "He fought in the Union army!"

Annie's brows knit together in a frown, making Charity feel obliged to expound upon her explanation.

She met the old woman's narrowed look. "Sam is a Southerner like me, and he wants to go back to Georgia." She shook her head sadly. "I couldn't marry a Yankee. I just couldn't! They burned my home, killed both my brother and the man I was goin' to marry. And. . .and I can't even say in church what one of them tried to do to me!" She blinked back the hot tears springing to her eyes. That was the truth. And if Annie thought ill of her for saying it out loud, it couldn't be helped.

A kind, sad smile softened the wrinkles around Annie's mouth and eyes. "Ma chère, the war is over. Our Lord tells us we must forgive those who sin against us seventy times seven." Annie paused and breathed a deep sigh. Her knobby fingers gave Charity's a gentle squeeze. "I do not know who you should marry, or even *if* you should marry. But I *do* know one thing. You've got to scrub your heart clean of the past."

The past.

Those two little words conjured up scenes so terrible and so vivid they still assaulted Charity's every sense. Irritation chafed up her spine. She had tried to forgive—ever since Jericho prayed with her the evening he saved her from that Yankee soldier. But how could she forgive when she couldn't forget?

She slid her hands from Annie's grasp. "I don't know, Annie. I don't know if I can."

Annie reached into her skirt pocket and pulled out a little black Bible. She thumbed the pages, then stopped and began to read the verse from First Corinthians Charity had committed to memory when she was but a small girl. " 'And now abideth faith, hope, charity, these three; but the greatest of these is charity.'"

Annie closed the book, slipped it back into her pocket, and stood. "You must live up to your name, Charity. Unless your heart is scrubbed clean of all malice, it won't be a fit place for God's love to grow."

Charity rose and picked up her satchel. She followed the old woman out of the pew and gave her a wan smile. "I will try, Annie."

When Charity stepped out of the church, the cold wind smacked her face like the truth in Annie's words. She headed down the steep slope of Perry Street toward home, her heart heavier than when she'd left the schoolhouse. Had she truly tried to forgive? She thought she had. Wasn't shoving thoughts of the war out of her mind and settling into a life here the same as putting the past behind her? Wasn't that a kind of forgiving?

Charity knew the answer. There was a part of her heart that had refused to relinquish the hurt and the rancor.

By the time she reached her aunt and uncle's home, she knew what she had to do. Lucy Morgan had been kind enough to invite her to her engagement party. It was a small step, but perhaps a step in the right direction. Charity would attend the party, even if the thought of attending another social event with Daniel Morgan made her heart tremble.

eleven

"Lucy's doll."

At his aunt's quiet voice, Daniel straightened suddenly from lounging against the piano in his parent's parlor. With the considerable crowd milling around the room, he hadn't noticed Aunt Rosaleen settle herself on the stool in front of the instrument's keyboard.

He and his aunt had always enjoyed a special relationship since the role he played in her rescue from a riverboat gambler when he was six. But following the *Sultana* disaster, the bond between them had grown even closer with their common experiences as survivors of separate steamboat explosions.

His aunt nodded, her look directed across the room where Daniel's gaze had been fixed for the past several minutes. "Miss Langdon—she reminds me of the china doll Lucy had when she was little. Don't you remember? The one with the blond hair."

Daniel did remember. The doll had been as delicate-looking as Charity. He even remembered it having a fancy blue dress—not so different from the blue party frock Charity was wearing this evening.

Daniel's gaze followed his aunt's. "Yes, I guess she does look something like that doll—except Charity is much prettier."

"Charity, hmm?" Aunt Rosaleen's teasing tone sent heat marching up Daniel's neck, making him wish he hadn't used Charity's given name. "I'm planning to play another waltz. Why don't you ask her to dance?" She gave his arm an encouraging pat. "You're supposed to be her escort, and the girl has danced with every male here but you, including John and Rory who seem to find dancing with Charity far preferable to dancing with their sisters or cousins." She added the last with a laugh as she glanced over at her fifteen-year-old twin sons who were helping themselves to the punch bowl.

Daniel cleared his throat. In truth, he didn't particularly care for social events and would have preferred to forego this one if he hadn't feared it might tarnish his sister's joy. That, and knowing Charity would be attending. "I don't know, Aunt Rosaleen." He tapped his bad leg. "I never danced well before I limped. Now...,"

"Nonsense! If you can walk, you can waltz." Aunt Rosaleen's blue-green eyes flashed. Daniel had learned through the years to heed his Uncle Jacob's oft-expressed warning, "When Rosaleen gets her Irish up, beware!"

Aunt Rosaleen's slender fingers slid expertly over the piano keys, executing a musical scale. She glanced across the room at Charity, who stood near the front window chatting with Lucy and Travis, then gave Daniel's back a gentle shove. "Now you go over there and ask her for the next dance before one of your cousins beats you to it."

Daniel gave his aunt a grin of surrender. "As you please, Aunt," he said with a chuckle and started across the parlor. He had no idea how his invitation might be received, so he was glad Aunt Rosaleen had begun playing a few scales to nimble her fingers. Hopefully, the sound would drown out the thumping of his heart.

He and Charity had exchanged only a handful of words since they boarded the train for Madison this morning. Though polite and cordial, her demeanor toward him had remained decidedly cool. Beyond the obligatory pleasantries common etiquette demanded, she'd opted to spend the train trip engrossed in a penny magazine rather than conversation with him. Upon their arrival, she'd spoken to him only to confirm the time of the party before Jericho escorted her to his home where Charity would be staying the night.

He would ask for the dance to please Aunt Rosaleen, but Daniel crossed the room with low expectations and high trepidation.

Suddenly Charity turned from talking to Lucy and Travis and looked directly at him. Her mouth wore the remnants of smile—probably in response to one of his future brother-in-law's famous jokes.

In that instant, Charity's beauty simply took his breath away.

Before Daniel could find his voice, Lucy piped up. "Daniel, you old stick-in-the-mud, you really must try to be more sociable!" Her brows pushed down into a perturbed V, but a light giggle danced through her words.

He hunched his shoulders and gave his sister the most innocent look he could muster. "Talking to Aunt Rosaleen doesn't count as being sociable?"

"Oh, you know what I mean," Lucy said with a huff. "Sometimes you act positively ancient, standing around talking to the old folks."

Charity's lips pressed tight together as if to stifle a giggle. The twinkle Daniel glimpsed in her blue eyes before she glanced away caused his heart to throb and his face to burn. Did she, too, think him stodgy?

Daniel looked toward the piano where his Uncle Jacob had joined Aunt Rosaleen. Standing close behind her with his hands on her shoulders, Uncle Jacob bent forward. With his cheek against his wife's, and his blond head pressed against her reddish-brown hair, they seemed to be studying the sheet music together.

"Old folks? I don't know, sis. They look pretty spry to me."

This time, Charity's giggle burst free.

Daniel garnered his courage and turned his attention from Lucy to Charity. "Speaking of my Aunt Rosaleen, Miss Langdon," he began, "I have it on very good authority that she is about to play a waltz. Would you do me the honor of partnering me for the dance?"

A look akin to panic flashed briefly across her face and his heart pinched. Perhaps she did find him distasteful. But then, a sweet smile bloomed on her features, and it was as if the sun had risen inside him. "I would be honored, sir," she said with a demure dip of her head.

A moment later, the melody of the waltz filled the parlor, and couples began twirling and gliding over the polished wood floor to the three-quarter tempo of a Strauss waltz.

Daniel's first few movements were stiff and unsure. He hadn't danced since before the war. He prayed he wouldn't tread on Charity's toes or step on the hem of her dress and rip it. He could feel beads of sweat break out at his temples. What a clod she must think him!

He felt compelled to voice an excuse in advance of any possibly embarrassing faux pas. "I hope you will pardon my clumsiness. It's been a long time since I've danced." He was acutely aware of her hand in his and the warmth of her tiny waist against his arm.

"You're doin' fine." Her encouraging smile filled him with relief. Perhaps his feet couldn't dance, but that smile of hers set his heart waltzing.

For a while they danced without further conversation. Having slipped more comfortably into the rhythm of the steps, Daniel simply enjoyed holding Charity in his arms. He silently blessed his aunt for prodding him toward this blissful moment.

As the dance entered its final movement, Charity's uptilted face held both surprise and appreciation. "Why Mr. Morgan, you were bein' far too modest. Your dancin' skills are superb. How long has it been since you last waltzed?"

"I suppose it was at my engagement party five years ago."

An odd expression crossed her face, and Daniel regretted having divulged that information.

Just then, the waltz ended, forcing him to reluctantly release her. He bowed deeply toward her, his heart feeling as bereft as his arms. "Thank you for the dance, Miss Langdon. I enjoyed it immensely."

She dipped a quick curtsy. "Thank you," she murmured.

Before she could say anything more, John and Rory appeared, plying her with cups of punch and each begging her for the next dance. One on either side of her, they bore her off toward the refreshment table.

Feeling oddly out of place, Daniel glanced around the room. Lucy and Travis had gone to sit together on the settee against the east wall, where they seemed to be engaged in intimate conversation. Mother and Pa were chatting with Uncle Jacob and Aunt Rosaleen by the piano. They were soon joined by his cousins, Lydia and Rose, and their husbands. Everyone seemed to have someone.

Perhaps it was the mention of his failed engagement, but for whatever reason, a wave of melancholy rippled through Daniel, and he found himself longing for a few moments of solitude.

Slipping out of the room, he headed for the hallway.

The library's open doors invited. He stepped into the darkened room and paused to light the oil lamp on the desk just inside the door. The warm, golden glow infused the space, illuminating its familiar comforts.

His gaze roamed the many bookshelves that lined the walls. How many blissful hours had he spent here as a boy, escaping to the exciting and wondrous worlds of Robinson Crusoe, Moby Dick, and Gulliver? But tonight he found no escape from the dispiriting feelings gripping him. This room, filled with so many memories, served only to accentuate his loneliness.

Crossing the braided rug that covered the center of the floor, he peered, unseeing, through the darkened window that divided the southern wall. A parade of memories marched before his mind's eye.

His spirit further deflated with the long, slow breath he expelled through his nostrils. Maybe Lucy was right. Maybe he was growing old and stodgy after all.

The sound of light footfalls along the hallway dragged him from his glum reverie. Lucy or Mother must be coming to fetch him back down to the party.

But when the footsteps continued down the hall and he heard the door to Mother's sitting room squeak open, he breathed a relieved sigh. Lucy had probably gone to find the latest edition of *Godey's Lady's Book* to share with their cousins.

In another moment, the footsteps resumed then stopped at the library's open door. He turned, resigned to be dragged back to the party by his determined sibling. But it was Charity, not his sister, he saw framed in the wide doorway, and his heart did a quick flip.

"I forgot and left my reticule on the table in the sewin' room when Lucy was showin' me and your cousins pictures of the latest weddin' gown styles." She held out her arm to display the little black beaded bag dangling from her wrist.

Struck momentarily mute, Daniel stood gazing at her, his eyes unable to get their fill of the sight. In the soft light of the oil lamp, Charity Langdon looked like a golden, satin-clad angel.

Just as she made a motion to turn, seemingly poised to head back to the parlor, she turned back to him, lingering. "Lucy was wonderin' where you had gone."

"Tell Lucy I'll be along shortly," he managed, finally finding his voice. He tried not to think of how wonderful Charity had felt in his arms during their shared waltz.

She nodded and sent him a shy smile, and his heart galloped. "Well, Jericho should be along directly to fetch me, so I should be gettin' back. . . ." Suddenly, her smile evaporated, and she seemed to focus on something past him near the floor. "My mother had a trunk just like that one." As if drawn to the thing, she stepped into the room and walked to the trunk beneath the window.

Daniel glanced down at the dome-topped spruce trunk. "It's just full of old keepsakes." He remembered when Pa had bought it in '47 for the family's trip to Promise, Indiana, to visit his Aunt Susannah, Mother's younger sister. He thought again of the fun he'd had playing around the Whitewater Canal near his aunt's inn while the family awaited the birth of his cousin, Georgiana.

"Ours held keepsakes, too—Mamma's weddin' dress that I'd planned to wear and things for my hope chest."

Something in Charity's voice told him her mother's trunk no longer existed. Her sad smile nearly broke his heart. "It was lost in the fire."

"I'm sorry." The two words seemed so insipid. . .so inadequate. But it was all he had to offer.

"Who was she—the girl to whom you were engaged?"

Daniel blinked at the unexpected question. "Phoebe Saunders—Bryant now."

"She's still alive?" Charity's confused look caused him to smile. Surely she didn't find it so incredible to imagine a young lady breaking off an engagement to him.

"Oh yes. Very much alive, married, and, to my understanding, the mother of four children." His grin widened. "Phoebe seemed to come to the conclusion that it would be far more prudent to marry a banker too nearsighted for the army than a man with perfect sight, who might not return from the war."

"I—I'm sorry." Charity's flustered demeanor thrilled Daniel more than the sentiment.

"Don't be. I've come to realize she did us both a favor." Daniel wished he could add that he'd only fully understood that truth since he'd met Charity.

"I was engaged once, too." Her quavering smile accompanying her admission suggested that unlike Phoebe, her intended was no longer living.

"And your intended. . . ?" The words crept out cautiously. He was sure he knew the answer but thought it only polite to inquire.

"He fell alongside my brother, Asa, at the Battle of Peachtree Creek."

"I'm sorry." This time when he muttered the trite condolence it chafed against his conscience. He was indeed sorry for the grief she'd borne. But he couldn't make his heart sorry that circumstances had rendered her unattached.

She nodded mutely, her gaze sliding back down to the trunk. "So many times I've wished we could have at least saved Mamma's trunk. But we—Jericho, Tunia, Pearl, and I—had only enough time to save ourselves and grab a few keepsakes and essentials before the fire took the house. I saved my mother's picture and her weddin' ribbons, but the rest. . . ."

Charity's delicate chin quivered as tears welled in her eyes and spilled down her cheeks, obliterating Daniel's restraint. He drew her into his embrace, muffling her soft sobs against his chest. As he rocked her in his arms, he sensed her tears were for far more than an old steamer trunk and its contents.

"I'm sorry. I'm so very, very sorry," he murmured against the sweet-smelling softness of her hair. Wishing he could offer her more in the way of comfort than the ridiculous sentiment, an unexpected prayer lifted from his heart.

Dear Lord, just help me know how to comfort her.

The next moment, she gently pushed away from him and lifted her tear-streaked face to his. Her long, honey-colored lashes still glistened with moisture while her petal-pink lips beckoned. A look of sweet understanding passed between them, presenting Daniel with a temptation he felt powerless to resist. He lowered his head, and her soft, sweet lips welcomed his.

In the midst of their tender kiss, Daniel found a joy beyond any he'd ever known—and with it, a new purpose and a new prayer. From this day forward, all he wanted from life was to love, comfort, and care for Charity Langdon.

Suddenly, she pushed hard away from him, ripping his heart asunder along with their embrace. She said nothing, but the look of horror and disgust on her face spoke agonizing volumes.

Watching her flee the room, Daniel was left in tortured confusion, his head spinning and his heart writhing.

twelve

"I cannot imagine what possessed me!" Charity stabbed the needle into the red wool material with unnecessary ferocity. "I should have known such a bright color would hurt my eyes when I chose it."

Aunt Jennie looked up from the tatting work in her hands. "You said red is the boy's favorite color. And red *is* traditional for Christmas."

Charity dropped the half-finished coat she was making for Henry into her lap and rubbed her eyes. Lately, it seemed everything set her nerves on edge. And she didn't like the feeling one bit.

"I could have Sarah Kerns finish it." Aunt Jennie's offer tiptoed out tentatively. "According to Iris, she does excellent work, and—"

"No!" Charity felt ashamed when her barked word made Aunt Jennie jump. She quickly tempered her tone. "I'm sorry, Aunt Jennie. This is my Christmas gift to Henry, and I should finish it myself. It's just that it gets dark so soon now, and this color is hard to work with in the lamplight."

Aunt Jennie narrowed her eyes at Charity and pursed her lips. "I must say, I don't know what to make of you these days, Charity. You've been in a sour mood ever since you returned from Madison. I trust Dr. Morgan and his family were in no way inhospitable to you."

"No. No, of course not. Dr. Morgan and his family were most congenial," Charity muttered.

Hoping to put an end to Aunt Jennie's troubling questions, Charity popped up from her sewing chair, draped the wool material over the chair's arm, and walked to one of the room's twin fireplaces. She picked up the iron poker and jabbed at the glowing maple logs in the hearth, feeding them oxygen and coaxing a renewed blaze from them. The smoke filled her nostrils and lungs, making her cough. But she welcomed the fire's heat scorching her face and giving her a reason to have flushed cheeks.

In truth, she knew all too well the cause of her ill humor. She'd been unable to get Daniel Morgan or their shared kiss off her mind in the week since she'd returned to Vernon. That she'd allowed such a thing to happen constituted only part of her shame. The fact that she'd enjoyed the kiss—had welcomed it—compounded her mortification. The night Jericho bashed that Yankee soldier in the head, saving her from an unthinkable fate, she vowed she would die before letting another Yankee touch her in such an intimate way. It had been the sudden memory of that vow washing through her on a wave of humiliation that had propelled her from Daniel's arms.

The pain she'd glimpsed in his dark eyes still gouged at her conscience. His intentions had been chaste, she had no doubt. In that brief moment of forgetfulness, she'd experienced a flash of unimagined joy. But the next moment, the past had intruded, rising between them like a dark and sinister specter.

And so it would always be. As kind, gentle, and caring as Daniel Morgan was, she feared there'd always be a part of her heart that would find him contemptible.

She'd stayed an extra day with the Emanuels so she wouldn't have to travel back to Vernon on the same train with Daniel. Thankfully, since her return to Vernon, she'd been too busy with her teaching job and helping Aunt Jennie around the house to spend any time at the mill. After Pearl left Uncle Silas and Aunt Jennie's employ, they'd had a series of housemaids, each staying only a few days. At present, they were once again without domestic help.

Aunt Jennie's voice penetrated her reverie. "I know it will

be a lot of extra work, but I'm glad you invited Mr. Porter and his little boy for Christmas. Having a child here will make the day more festive, don't you think?"

Charity hurried to agree, glad that her aunt had abandoned the subject of Charity's latest trip to Madison.

"I actually enjoyed the little lad's company at Thanksgiving, despite the unfortunate accident with your mother's picture," Aunt Jennie said with a soft laugh.

"I'd nearly forgotten." Charity crossed to the little mahogany table. "I want to buy a new frame for Mamma's picture."

She opened the table drawer and gave a little gasp. The picture, frame and all, was gone. Down to the last shard of broken glass.

"Aunt Jennie. Did you move Mamma's picture?"

Her aunt craned her neck around, her face full of surprise. "Why no, dear. It's not there?"

"No," Charity breathed the word softly. She continued to stare at the empty drawer, as if by looking hard enough she might cause the picture to materialize.

Aunt Jennie's brow puckered. "I recall asking Deloris. . .you remember Deloris, don't you? She was the second housemaid after Pearl left."

Charity gave an impatient nod, and Aunt Jennie resumed her disjointed thought. "Anyway, I had the woman pack away several pieces of bric-a-brac to make room for Christmas decorations. She must have found the picture in the drawer and packed it away in one of the boxes."

Aunt Jennie's shoulders rose and fell in an unconcerned shrug. "I'm sure that's where it is, but I'm afraid we must wait until after Christmas to look for it. Silas would not be well pleased to have to fetch those boxes down from the attic then carry them back up again."

Charity's heart ached. She could only pray her aunt was right. The thought of losing such a dear memento was crushing. She returned to her sewing, determined to climb to the attic and search for herself at first opportunity.

Exhaling a soft sigh, Charity took her work back upon her lap, then reached across the table beside her chair and turned up the wick on the kerosene lamp. She wasn't even half done with Henry's coat. And with school and helping Aunt Jennie with Christmas preparations crowding her days, Charity would have little time for snooping in the attic.

As she worked the bright thread around a buttonhole, Charity's mood lifted with her smile. Like Aunt Jennie, she looked forward to Henry's presence at Christmas. Although she'd stopped accepting Sam Porter's attentions, she could not bear to distance herself from the little boy who'd become dear to her. Having noticed the ragged state of his patched coat, she'd decided to make him a new one. It warmed her heart to imagine his shrieks of glee when he discovered his new red coat on Christmas Day. She was smiling at the thought when several sharp raps at the front door yanked both her and Aunt Jennie's attentions across the parlor to the hallway.

"I'll get it." Once more, Charity rose and set her needlework aside. Hopefully, it was the woman Iris Pemberton most recently recommended as a possible housemaid.

But when Charity opened the door, her heart shot right to her throat. Daniel stood on the porch, the December wind batting the brim of his slouch hat.

"I just returned from taking a load of corn to the depot. As it is the end of the day, I thought I'd bring by the bill of lading." He looked everywhere but her face.

Charity reached for the square of yellow paper he held out to her, careful not to allow their hands to touch during the transfer.

"Might I come in? I'd like a word or two with Mr. Gant, if he's here." At last, his gaze settled on hers.

"Yes—yes, of course," she murmured, embarrassed by her lapse of manners. "Uncle Silas is in the library." She shuffled backwards a couple of steps, making room for him in the cramped space. Her pulse raced. She hadn't been this close to Daniel since that evening in the library at his parents' home.

He dragged off his hat and twisted it in his large hands. His gaze skittered away from hers again, and she suspected his mind, too, had returned to the moment of their warm embrace.

"Charity. . . ." Her name drifted out on a slowly exhaled breath, and his dark eyes looked deeply into hers. "I want to apologize—"

"No apology needed, Mr. Morgan." Her heart throbbing, Charity feigned a light tone. "I'm sure Uncle Silas will be glad to talk with you." She then whirled around and led him down the short hallway. She knew well he wasn't referring to his unannounced appearance. But she couldn't bear to hear him say he was sorry he had kissed her.

After leaving Daniel in the library with her uncle, Charity rejoined her aunt in the parlor. Unable to concentrate on her sewing, she managed only a few stitches while keeping her ears perked for footfalls in the hallway.

A few minutes later, she heard Uncle Silas's and Daniel's unintelligible voices and their footsteps moving toward the back of the house. A thread of disappointment wove through her. What was the matter with her? Why should she long for another glimpse of Daniel Morgan when she'd been avoiding him at all costs since her return from Madison?

She jabbed the needle into the wool. When its point struck her finger, she emitted a soft cry of pain.

"Be careful, my dear," Aunt Jennie chided gently. "Perhaps you should use a thimble."

Charity continued her work in sullen silence, wishing there was such a thing as a thimble for the heart.

thirteen

"Where do you go, Daniel, when you look off into that place the rest of us can't see?"

Uncle Jacob's quiet words pulled Daniel back to his parents' parlor. Grinning, he turned to his uncle and accepted the mug of hot apple cider he held out to him. He inhaled the fragrant steam spiraling from the mulled drink. "Sorry," he murmured, wishing his uncle wasn't so perceptive.

Uncle Jacob settled himself on the sofa across from Daniel's chair and breathed a contented sigh. "You've been staring at that Christmas tree for ten minutes, and I'll wager you couldn't tell me if Lucy got her way and topped it with an angel, or my Rose won the argument and a star sits on its highest branch."

Unwilling to admit that his mind had indeed been absent, traveling unbidden back to Vernon, Daniel decided an evasive maneuver was the best tactic. "I didn't think preachers were supposed to gamble, Uncle Jacob," he said and sipped the warm, spicy cider.

"You know very well I meant it only as an expression. Don't change the subject. And no fair peeking." Uncle Jacob's blue eyes sparkled with fun.

Daniel averted his eyes from the spruce tree in the front corner of the parlor. He, Pa, Uncle Jacob, and Travis had spent the better part of the morning scouring the wooded hills on the north side of Madison for the two best-looking young spruces they could find. One now graced the front parlor of Uncle Jacob and Aunt Rosaleen's parsonage. The other stood across the room, being adorned in festive splendor by Lucy, Travis, and Daniel's cousins. From an adjacent settee, Mother and Aunt Rosaleen offered the enthusiastic young workers suggestions as to how they might best proceed.

"Why, it's an angel, of course, Uncle." Daniel gave Uncle Jacob a sly grin. "You know Lucy always gets her way."

A rich, throaty chuckle burst from Uncle Jacob's lips. "That she does," he admitted, his attention turning to Lucy, who stood laughing with her intended across the room. "The poor fellow had no idea his fate was sealed the moment your sister set her cap for him."

Daniel watched Lucy and Travis argue playfully over the placement of a brightly colored glass bulb. At another time, his uncle's comment might have brought an easy grin to his face. But not now. Not with the rich smell of pine in his nostrils, the taste of spiced cider on his tongue, and the dazzle of Christmas brilliance all around him. Instead, his mouth drooped with his heart. To his shame, he felt a wave of envy swell up in his chest.

He wrapped both hands around the warm cup of cider and gazed into its amber contents. "Oh, I don't know, Uncle. I'd say Travis is one lucky man."

"That he is, Daniel." The smile in Uncle Jacob's voice faded, and Daniel could sense his elder's gaze. "Hmm," he murmured in that knowing tone that warned Daniel his thoughts had been breached. "That brings us back to where we were, doesn't it?"

Daniel said nothing as he studied the tiny brown specks of grated cinnamon floating in his cider. There was no use in trying to evade Uncle Jacob's dogged curiosity.

"You know," Uncle Jacob's voice lifted, "just this past week I joined two couples in marriage. And each of those four people had either passed a fortieth birthday or was nearing it. You are still a very young man, Daniel. I have no doubt there is someone out there for you."

Daniel's mouth twisted in a wry grin. If only his problem was as simple as desiring to find a wife. Such an obscure longing didn't approach the anguish of having lost his heart to one who considered him repugnant.

"Ah, I see." Uncle Jacob dragged out the words in a low tone of enlightenment. "Miss Langdon, I presume?"

Daniel nodded. His jaw jerked with a feeble smile. "I'm afraid she finds me. . .distasteful. I assume because I wore the Union uniform."

His uncle reached over and tapped the knee of his bad leg. "Does she know about Andersonville?"

"No." Daniel's scalp prickled at the name of the place. He didn't like to think about it, let alone hear the word spoken. Daniel's spirit ebbed with his sigh, and he shook his head. "Maybe it's just as well, Uncle Jacob. There are so many memories—bad ones—on each side. I don't know how it would ever work."

"Daniel,"—Uncle Jacob reached over and patted Daniel's knee—"with God, all things are possible. God allowed this girl to set your heart alight for a reason. Maybe it's to be your helpmate, and maybe it's for an altogether different purpose. Let God guide you, Daniel. Don't close your mind, or heart, to any possibilities."

Daniel noticed Aunt Rosaleen had gone to the piano and begun softly playing a carol. A shuffling sound in the hall drew his attention to the parlor doorway. Pa, who had left sometime earlier to deliver a Christmas Eve baby, stood smiling at his family. Snowflakes still clung to his hat and caped shoulders. His arms were filled with several brightly wrapped packages.

Amid squeals from the girls, Mother rushed to give him a tender kiss and divest him of some of the colorful bundles.

At the sight, Daniel's heart throbbed with a sense of loneliness. How was Charity spending her Christmas Eve? Would she like the gift he made for her, or would she take offense?

When he joined his family around the piano to sing, "It Came Upon the Midnight Clear," Daniel marveled at how such an idyllic scene could seem incomplete. How he longed to have Charity by his side, gazing up at him adoringly as Lucy was doing to Travis.

As he sang the words of the song's third verse, they convicted his heart.

> Yet with the woes of sin and strife
> The world has suffered long;
> Beneath the angel strain have rolled
> Two thousand years of wrong;
> And man, at war with man, hears not
> The love-song which they bring;
> O hush the noise, ye men of strife
> And hear the angels sing.

Charity cared for him, he was sure of it. He'd felt it in her kiss. He'd seen it in her eyes. The war was over. If he could put it behind him, so could she. He vowed to return to Vernon with a renewed resolve to win her heart.

fourteen

"For me?" The light in Henry's wide eyes as he unwrapped the red wool coat and cap Charity had made for him set her heart aglow.

"Of course," Charity said with a laugh. It certainly wouldn't fit anyone else here."

Henry wasted no time in shrugging on the coat and plopping the cap on his head.

Charity, her aunt and uncle, and Sam and Henry had just moved from the dining room to the parlor following a sumptuous Christmas dinner. Thankfully, two weeks ago, Aunt Jennie had hired a widow and her fifteen-year-old daughter to help with the cooking and other domestic chores.

It had thrilled Charity to watch Henry enjoy the meal. In fact, all morning her heart had warmed seeing the wonder and joy glowing from his little face. Several times during the Christmas service at church this morning, she'd questioned the wisdom of encouraging the child's attachment to her. Clearly, he had begun to see her more as a mother figure than simply a teacher.

And it wasn't just Henry. Sam, too, had shown signs of having been emboldened by her invitation for him and Henry to join her and the Gants for Christmas. She'd done her best not to encourage him, addressing him only by his surname and keeping Henry between them in the church pew. And she'd been adamant that she would ride to and from church with Uncle Silas and Aunt Jennie. But despite her efforts to dampen his ardor, Sam's attentions toward her had intensified.

But looking at Henry's happy face, she knew she'd made the right decision. She'd had the power to make the little boy's

Christmas a delight instead of the dismal day he would have most likely spent otherwise.

"Look, Pa, look at my new coat and hat!" Henry scampered over to Sam then pulled up short as if remembering himself.

"That's mighty fine, boy. Mighty fine." Sam's eyes held little warmth when he spoke to his son, a reaction Charity had noticed several times before. It also bothered her that she'd never heard Sam call Henry "son." His distant demeanor seemed to keep the child at arm's length. "Now show some manners, boy, and thank Miss Langdon for her gift." The odd look on Sam's face sent warning bells clanging inside Charity. Did that little smirk suggest he saw Henry as a way to her heart?

Henry proceeded to do just that, throwing his little arms around Charity's waist in an affection-starved hug. Although Henry received several other gifts, including marbles and two school tablets from Uncle Silas and Aunt Jennie and a Barlow knife from Sam, his favorite present was clearly the new coat and hat. He refused to take them off, even when beads of sweat popped out on his forehead.

As evening approached, sending shadows stretching across the parlor, conversation waned. Only the crackling and popping of the fireplaces and Uncle Silas snoring in his chair disturbed the silence.

At length, Aunt Jennie daintily stifled a yawn with her fingertips and rose from her chair. "Come, Henry." She reached a hand out to the child playing with his marbles on the floor. "Let's go ask Mrs. Akers and Matilda to wrap up some of those iced cookies for you to take home."

Henry quickly stuffed the marbles into his new coat pocket, then scrambled to Aunt Jennie's side and took her hand.

Charity found herself in the uncomfortable position of sitting alone on the sofa beside Sam with only her sleeping uncle as chaperone. Rising, she gave a nervous little laugh. "Perhaps I should go help Aunt Jennie and Henry with those cookies."

"I will not." He grasped her arm, compelling her to sit back down. "I'd like a few words with you."

The serious look on Sam's face filled Charity with trepidation. Feeling like a rabbit cornered by a fox, she forced herself to not bolt for the kitchen.

He reached inside his coat and pulled out a pamphlet. "There's a new South bein' built, Charity." He waved the paper beneath her nose. "Land can be bought for a fraction of what it would have cost before the war. We could go back—you, me, and Henry—we could start anew."

Charity leaned farther away from him, repelled by his suggestion. She, too, had seen the advertisements—publications put out by carpetbaggers looking to profit from selling stolen lands back to displaced Southerners. "Sam, I—I'm not prepared to speak of such things."

The scowl drawing his brows into a V disappeared as quickly as it had come. He stuffed the pamphlet back into his coat. "I understand. I'm gettin' ahead of myself. First things first."

Brightening, he reached back into his coat pocket and pulled out a small pewter box. "I have somethin' for you that I saved until. . . ." He glanced at Uncle Silas, whose bottom jaw sagged as he continued to snore loudly. "Until we were somewhat alone."

Charity's heart quaked. As much as she would like to be Henry's mother, her every instinct rebelled against becoming Sam's wife. "Really, Mr. Porter, I cannot—"

"Nonsense. Of course you can. You and your kin have been more than generous with me and my boy. At least allow me to give you this little token of my affection." He flipped open the hinged box to reveal a gold locket necklace.

Gazing at the piece of jewelry, Charity felt only one emotion—anger. It was obvious that Henry didn't eat as well as he should. He wore tattered and patched clothes to school, and his boots looked a half-size too small with soles worn nearly paper-thin. How dare this man allow his own son to go wanting while he bought expensive trinkets for the object of his affection?

Charity took the box, snapped it closed, and handed it back to Sam. "It's a lovely gesture, and I do appreciate the thought. But I can't accept it. I would much rather you return the necklace and use the money to buy Henry a new pair of boots."

Sam's face reddened. His jaw hardened, and anger flashed from his eyes like barbed lightning. For a moment, Charity feared he might strike her. He shoved the box back into his coat pocket and shot to his feet. "I doubt you would have turned it down if that Yankee, Morgan, had offered it!"

Charity opened her mouth but could think of nothing to say that might calm him.

Sam's hands balled at his sides in fists. "Forgive me, ma'am. I mistook you for a Southern lady. I see you're nothing but a Yankee-lover," he said, grinding the words through his clenched jaw.

Just that moment, Aunt Jennie and Henry appeared in the parlor.

Sam glanced at Henry who was lugging a linen-covered basket with both hands. "Gather your things, boy. I fear we may have overstayed our welcome." Although he seemed to make a mighty effort to temper his tone in Aunt Jennie's presence, his voice still grated with a hard edge.

By the time Charity had Henry's new coat all buttoned up, Sam managed to get control of his voice. Aunt Jennie woke Uncle Silas and they all bunched in the front hallway. There, Sam delivered his thanks and goodbyes in the smooth, sugary tones of a Southern gentleman.

But all the while, fear, anger, and disgust knotted in Charity's chest. Now she understood the look of fear she'd seen in Henry's eyes when Sam spoke to him. She'd experienced it firsthand.

"Miss Langdon." Sam's voice was sweet as his head bent

to brush a kiss across the back of her hand, but the look of smoldering fury in his eyes stunned her.

She quickly pulled her hand away and crouched to give Henry a warm hug. "Be a good boy, Henry," she whispered in his ear. "And don't forget to say your prayers. Remember, if you're ever afraid, just pray and ask Jesus to take care of you, and He will."

Henry gave her a solemn nod and Charity's heart twisted.

She stood at the open door and watched the mule-drawn wagon bear father and son down Perry Street through the purple-tinted winter dusk. Would Sam take out his anger toward her on Henry? She fought down the panic bubbling up inside of her at the thought.

Dear Jesus, just protect him. Protect little Henry.

When she finally shut the door, a tap on her shoulder turned her around. Uncle Silas was holding a flat package wrapped in brown paper. "I forgot, niece, there was one more gift for you," he said with an odd smile as he handed her the package.

"Thank you, Uncle Silas." She tried to force a smile. Whatever the gift was, it seemed unimportant after sending that sweet little boy off with an angry father who was capable of... what? She didn't like to imagine.

Uncle Silas held both hands up, palms forward. "Don't thank me. I'm only playing St. Nick." Uncle Silas's rosy cheeks above his graying mustache plumped up with his smile, bringing an easier grin to Charity's face. If anyone looked the part, it was certainly Uncle Silas.

He lifted his overcoat and hat from the row of wall pegs. "Now, I must hitch up the buggy and take Mrs. Akers and her daughter home. Probably with enough food to keep them through the next week, if I know Jennie." With a little laugh, he sauntered off toward the kitchen.

Charity followed her uncle around the L-shaped hallway toward the stairs. She could hear Aunt Jennie, Sadie, and Matilda Akers chatting as they worked in the kitchen. She would take the gift—most likely a token from the school board—up to her bedroom and open it later.

Up in her room, she dropped the wrapped package on the table by her bed and started to turn and head back downstairs. But in the dim, flickering light from the fireplace, the name Daniel on the right top corner of the package caught her eye.

She lit the oil lamp on the table, sat down on the edge of her bed, and picked up the package. Sure enough, clearly penciled in Daniel Morgan's handwriting was "To Charity from Daniel."

She tore away the brown paper, and her heart nearly stopped. In her hands lay her mother's picture she'd feared had been lost. But now it was encased in new glass and a beautifully hand-carved walnut frame.

Charity ran a finger lovingly over the rose and leaf design delicately etched in the wood. He'd done this. She didn't doubt it for an instant. She couldn't begin to guess the hours it must have taken him to create this stunning piece of art—all for her.

Charity's eyes stung, and her mother's image blurred. Sam was right. She loved Daniel Morgan. She could no longer deny it. Yet her mind stubbornly rebelled against the notion of a romantic relationship with a former Yankee soldier. The tears that had slowly welled suddenly became a torrent, and she sobbed. She held her mother's picture to her heart and rocked herself on the edge of her bed as tears streamed down her face.

"Dear Lord, what am I to do? What am I to do?"

fifteen

"Thank you."

Charity's soft voice behind him caught Daniel up short in midstride. He'd been on his way to shut the sluice gate in preparation of closing the mill for the day.

"For the frame you made for my mother's picture, thank you. It's beautiful." It wasn't so much her words or quiet voice as the way her gaze drifted shyly away from his that caused Daniel's heart to pound.

"I'm glad you liked it. I was afraid you might—might take offense. . . ." Daniel found himself almost mesmerized by the condensation of her warm breath in the cold mill. The misty clouds puffed from her rosy lips with her every breath—the essence of her. His arms ached to embrace her—to hold her close and warm against him.

"Not at all." The surprise on her face that told him such an idea had never crossed her mind set a surge of relief rolling through Daniel.

Her gaze continued to glance away from his. But he sensed her avoidance of his look was not generated by disdain. Indeed, the relief in his chest mingled with the sweet notion that her demeanor sprang from attraction rather than revulsion.

She seemed to study the fringes of her shawl, rolling one short length of wool thread between two fingers. "Had I known beforehand, I would have reciprocated in kind. . .in some small way. . . ."

Daniel prayed—something he'd been doing more of lately. Just this moment, he prayed that his throat wouldn't tighten up, strangling his voice to a croak. He shook his head and bought himself another second or two of time. "But don't you agree that if a gift is paid back, its value is made null, robbing the giver of the joy of having given the gift in the first place?"

She looked up at him. An appreciative smile, as slow and languid as her Southern accent, crept over her lips, and then a musical giggle bubbled from between them. "Why, Mr. Morgan, I had no idea you were such a philosopher."

"I've been called worse, I suppose," he blurted and silently upbraided himself for the stupid reply.

"Still, your thesis aside, I hope you will accept an invitation to dinner this Sunday." She pulled the dark wool shawl closer around her, forcing him to, again, resist the impulse to wrap her in his arms.

"I will agree on two conditions. You call me Daniel and allow me to escort you to church."

The words had flown from his lips before he realized his blunder. Since Christmas, Porter had been crowing about having spent Christmas Day with the Gants and the particular attention Charity had been giving his son, Henry. It was even possible Charity and Porter had an understanding. The thought raked across Daniel's heart like a briar.

To his utter relief, she gave him a smile and a nod, allowing him to breathe again. "I would be honored. . .Daniel."

She held out her hand to him and he enclosed it in his. It was the first time they had touched since the kiss.

Realization flickered in her eyes. Yet her gaze didn't waver from his, nurturing the hope growing in his heart.

"I will see you Sunday morning then." He held her hand a moment longer than convention allowed and felt the loss acutely when she slipped her fingers from his.

"This Sunday," she repeated, but her smile had faded. A troubled look flashed across her face. It seemed directed toward a point past his shoulder.

She turned abruptly and headed out of the mill. Her quick footsteps clicking against the wooden floor echoed his racing heart. Silas Gant wasn't here. And Charity hadn't gone to her little office. She had come to the mill for no other purpose than to thank him for the picture frame.

Through the window, Daniel watched her climb into the buggy and turn it toward the little gravel path. Was it indeed possible she could care for him? Could he trust this tiny glimmer of hope flickering inside of him?

He remembered the scripture from the Gospel of Mark Uncle Jacob reminded him of Christmas Eve. *"For with God all things are possible."*

During the war, he'd prayed daily. His connection with God had sustained him through the horrors of Andersonville. When he survived the sinking of the *Sultana* without being burned or suffering any other serious injuries, he'd considered it nothing less than a miracle from God. But oddly, the moment he reached the safety of home, he'd stopped praying, reading his Bible, or even going to church. He'd pushed God away along with all other recollections of the war. Uncle Jacob had reminded him that his need for God didn't end with the war. And suddenly, that need never seemed greater than at this moment.

Dear Lord, forgive me for neglecting You.

"The last grind has been bagged. So, with your permission, sir, I will be leavin' for the day." Sam Porter's voice behind Daniel was as chilly as the mill's interior.

Daniel turned to meet the man's scowl. He wondered if it was Porter's disgruntled look that had withered Charity's smile moments earlier.

"Thank you, Sam. . .and good evening." Daniel fought to push his mouth into what he hoped was a pleasant expression. Did the man actually see him as a possible contender for Charity's affection? Oddly, the thought buoyed his spirits.

He watched the Southerner swagger past him, ignoring the man's scornful snort. During his time in Andersonville, Daniel had learned that allowing an adversary to goad him into anger invariably handed his opponent the advantage. And Daniel had no doubt that in a contest where Charity Langdon's affections were the prize, he had a committed adversary in Sam Porter.

ॐ

"Daniel, I need your help." Charity glanced over at Daniel's profile beside her in the rented buggy. The ride to church was a short one, so she didn't have the luxury of leading up to the subject gradually. The surprise mixing with concern on his face would have caused her to smile if the situation weren't so serious.

For the past week, she had agonized over the bruises she'd noticed on Henry. Convinced that her worst fears on Christmas night had come true, she was desperate to save the child from further injury.

"Of course. I will help you in any way I can if it is within my power to do so." He kept the horse to a slow walk, which she sensed had less to do with the snow-covered streets than allowing extra time for their conversation.

"I think Sam Porter is beatin' Henry." There, she'd said it. In one awful rush of breath, she'd impugned the man she'd not so long ago considered marrying.

"What?" Daniel shot her a sidelong glance, his knuckles whitening around the leather reins. "Do you have any proof of this?"

Charity wadded the ends of her shawl in her hands and wished for Henry's sake she didn't have so much proof. She told Daniel about the bruises on the boy's face and hands. "He always has an excuse when I ask him what happened." Charity blinked back tears remembering how Henry had shrugged off her questions about an ugly purple bruise on his right cheek last Thursday. "He said he fell against a rick of wood when he went to fetch fuel for the stove."

"And you didn't believe him?" Although a frown continued to line his forehead, the doubt in his voice sent ripples of panic through Charity. If she couldn't find an ally in Daniel, where could she turn?

"Fallin' doesn't leave marks that resemble a man's fingers on a child's wrist!" she blurted, barely able to contain both her anger and her tears.

Daniel blew out a long breath. "No, it doesn't." The anger snapping in his dark eyes gave her hope. "Have you spoken to Mr. and Mrs. Gant about your concerns?"

"I tried." The words rolled out on a puff of frustration. Charity held out her hands to demonstrate her helplessness. "I could tell Aunt Jennie was concerned, but she shrinks from anything controversial. She simply said it is not our place to dictate how a father should deal with his son. And Uncle Silas just laughed and said boys are rambunctious and are always gettin' hurt."

Charity rested her hand on Daniel's arm. "I was hopin' that perhaps you could have a word with Sam. Mention how glad you are that you had a kind father. . .somethin'." She shook her head. "I'm worried sick about Henry, and I don't know where else to turn. And I think Sam might respond better to another man."

Transferring the reins to one hand, Daniel covered her hand on his arm with his free hand. His smile sent warm encouragement radiating through her. "Don't worry. I'll talk to Sam."

When they reached the churchyard and Daniel parked the buggy, he turned and took Charity's hands in his. His gaze caressed hers. Deep, dark pools of bottomless kindness she could get lost in. Could these be the eyes of one who'd glared in hatred at her loved ones across a battlefield? The thought seemed impossible.

The January wind tugged at her shawl and nipped at her cheeks, but she didn't care. She wanted to continue sitting there, soaking up the strength, the warmth, the security that flowed from Daniel's hands to hers.

"It will be all right," he said, and the assurance in his voice made her believe it. "In the meantime, let us pray that God will soften Sam's heart, or at the very least stay his hand if raised in anger against the boy."

And Charity did pray.

Throughout the church service, she found her attention constantly drifting from Reverend Davenport's sermon to Henry Porter's plight. It alarmed her to see that Sam and Henry were not present at services. She made a mental note to offer Henry a ride to church whether or not his father chose to attend. The thought that she could somehow protect Henry if she were to become his mother still tortured Charity.

She glanced at Daniel sitting next to her in the church pew, and her heart rebelled against such a sacrificial notion, however noble. It seemed a vile sin to vow to love, honor, and obey a man capable of injuring his own flesh and blood while her affections twined ever tighter around the good, decent man beside her.

❧

Monday brought Charity no relief from her worries. Henry didn't show up at school, leaving her to wonder if he lay too sick or injured to attend. Something was wrong. He was always one of the first to arrive in the morning and the last to leave in the afternoon.

Although frantic to learn of the boy's situation, Charity had a school full of other students to teach. She would have to wait until after school to check on Henry.

The day dragged as she spent every spare moment praying for Henry's safety and glancing at the excruciatingly slow-moving hands on the wall clock. When three thirty finally came and the last student had left, Charity rushed through the routine chores of closing the school for the day. She knew she wouldn't be able to sleep tonight if she didn't stop by the Porters' home and assure herself Henry was all right.

She'd just reached up to turn the damper on the stovepipe, cutting off the oxygen supply to the smoldering coals in the stove's iron belly, when she felt a draft of cold air behind her. One of the students must have forgotten something and returned.

She whirled around, her every muscle tensing with impatience at the shuffling sound near the door. "Yes, what is it—" The sight of Daniel in the doorway snatched the breath from her lungs. And the somber look on his face made her tremble.

"He quit." The two words rang hollowly in the empty room.

Charity could only stare at him. She didn't need to ask, "Who?"

"I'm sorry." He twisted his hat in his hands and shook his head. "I made a mess of it. I told Sam you were worried about the bruises you'd seen on his boy. He said he didn't need Yankees or Yankee-lovers telling him how to raise his son." Daniel's Adam's apple bobbed with his swallow. "He told me he was quitting, dropped what he was doing, and just walked out."

A new and terrible fear gripped Charity. For one awful moment, she couldn't move. She couldn't breathe. Sam would have been furious. And if Henry was home when Sam returned from the mill, Henry would most likely have borne the brunt of Sam's anger. What was worse, Charity knew she had brought it about. "Daniel." His name croaked from her frozen throat. "Henry didn't come to school today."

Daniel's face blanched. His gaze locked with hers in a grim, mutual understanding.

sixteen

"Let's go." Daniel snatched Charity's heavy wool shawl from the wall peg and draped it around her shoulders.

He felt sick. Porter had a hair-trigger temper, and Daniel had witnessed the man take his anger out on whatever hapless creature had the misfortune to be in his way. If he thought the boy had gone to Charity and Daniel for help. . .it didn't bear thinking.

"Daniel, it's not your fault. I asked you to talk to Sam. If it's anyone's fault, it's mine." Charity's words, puffing out in the cold air as he led her across the snowy schoolyard, touched Daniel deeply but did little to ease his guilt.

He helped her onto the wagon seat then climbed up beside her. Watching her fingers convulse, wadding handfuls of her skirt, he winced. He couldn't bear to see her blame herself for Henry's welfare. "Charity, if Sam's hurt that boy, it's nobody's fault but Sam's."

Charity nodded as he took off the brake and grasped the reins. Her delicate chin trembled, and Daniel vowed to make Sam pay if he'd hurt Henry.

They made the trip across Vernon in silence.

Perhaps Charity was wrong and Sam was lovingly caring for his son who'd woken up with a fever or a bellyache or. . .the quivering in Daniel's stomach told him that scenario wasn't likely.

At last, he pulled the wagon up in front of the little dilapidated hovel at the south end of Posey Street Sam and Henry called home. Daniel had learned from his landlady, Essie Kilgore, that few in Vernon had cared to rent to a Reb. But for the boy's sake, old man Gossman had rented Sam this empty shotgun shack not much larger than a summer kitchen.

Before Daniel could help her down, Charity clambered from the wagon and hurried to the house. Her sharp raps on the weathered front door went unanswered.

Daniel walked to the back corner of the house. He could see Sam's unsaddled horse munching on hay in the three-sided shed. He doubted the man had walked any distance through the several inches of snow cover.

He rejoined Charity at the front of the house. Her drooping shoulders as she turned from the door spoke of her disappointment at finding no one home. Daniel seriously considered trying the door, just to check on Henry and ease her mind.

Suddenly the door opened, releasing a stench composed of several foul odors. Not the least of which were whiskey, rancid lard, and kerosene.

"Whatcha want?" Sam swayed unsteadily in the open doorway. He was shirtless with the top half of his dingy underwear unbuttoned at the throat. His sagging galluses hung off his shoulders.

"I want to see Henry." Charity's plucky challenge made Daniel smile. Many women would have fled, scandalized by the man's condition of undress.

"He's not here. Ain't seen 'im since he left for school this mornin'. Dawdlin', most like."

Sam's bleary-eyed gaze drifted from Charity to Daniel and back to Charity again. He gave a soft snort. "So, Miss Langdon, you and your Yankee—"

"Stop right there, Porter!" Anger stiffened Daniel's spine and he stepped toward Sam. He would not allow this man's whiskey-soaked tongue to embarrass or impugn Charity in any way. "Your boy never showed up at school. Miss Langdon just came by to assure herself he is all right."

To his credit, Sam Porter seemed to sober slightly. "He wasn't at school?"

"No." The word quivered from Charity's lips, and she turned horror-widened eyes to Daniel.

The color drained from Porter's face, softening Daniel's opinion of him. Daniel gripped Sam's arm. "Do you know where your boy might have gone? Maybe to one of the neighbors'?"

Sam gave his head an emphatic shake. "No. I tanned him right good for doin' that once without tellin' me. He wouldn't do it again."

Daniel's voice rose. Trying to drag useful information from Sam's whiskey-soaked brain was beyond frustrating.

"Georgia," Sam suddenly muttered and looked like he might be sick. "I—I gave him a tannin' last night for sassin' me. He said he was goin' to leave and go back to Georgia." His gaze that swung from Daniel to Charity pled for understanding. "He's seven. I never thought he'd try. . . ."

Daniel strove to keep the disgust from his voice. "Get your clothes on, man. It'll be dark soon. We need to go after him." Drunk or sober, Sam Porter would have the best idea where to start looking for Henry.

Five minutes later, Sam, now fully clothed, led Charity and Daniel behind the house. He gave his head a quick jerk to the south. "Henry likes to play back here in the trees a lot."

Among dog and rabbit tracks that marred the snow cover, they could make out small human footprints leading to the narrow wooded area between the house and the river gorge. Beyond the tree line, the footprints were no longer obvious, obliterated by deepening shadows and myriad animal tracks. Daniel and Charity followed Sam's lead, dodging bare tree limbs and briars until they emerged at an open space overlooking the Muscatatuck River.

But they found no sign of Henry.

Just when Daniel was about to suggest they question the neighbors who lived a few yards behind them along East Jackson Street, Charity's excited voice stopped him.

"Here. Over here," she called from where she'd wandered westward along the edge of the woods.

Daniel rushed to join her with Sam close on his heels. He followed Charity's gaze to a stretch of snow-covered ground streaked alternately with the evening's lengthening purple shadows and the gold of the setting sun. There in the snow, he could make out a line of small footprints heading west and running parallel to the woods.

Charity repeatedly called the boy's name as she followed the trail of footprints.

Suddenly, a small figure dressed in red appeared from behind a large bush several yards ahead of them. The boy stood silhouetted against the snow, between the woods and the river gorge.

Sam took quick steps toward the boy. "Henry! Henry, you come here right now, boy, or I'll wear that strap out on you!"

When Henry took off in the opposite direction, Daniel couldn't blame him, but his heart quaked at the sight. The boy was running straight for the bluff where the land sloped steeply down to the river's edge. Recent rains had swollen the usually shallow, languid river, making it a rushing torrent. If Henry slipped and fell down the ten-foot slope and into the river, the current could easily carry him away before they could ever reach him.

The next moment, Daniel's worst fear was realized when Henry stumbled and fell and with a yelp, slid over the embankment and out of sight. An instant later, Daniel heard a splash.

Charity screamed Henry's name, and to Daniel's horror, he watched her follow Henry, disappearing down the incline.

Shouting Charity's name, Daniel raced to the spot where she and Henry had gone over the edge of the bluff. Beside him, and sounding just as frantic, Sam called for his son.

Daniel's heart sank when he saw no sign of them. Then the sound of splashing and fractured cries for help drew his attention to a spot several yards downstream. Squinting westward against the setting sun, he could make out Charity's head and upper torso. She seemed to be clinging with one hand to a partially submerged tree limb. With her other hand, she amazingly grasped something red from which poked a sputtering little head.

His mind numb with fear for both Charity and the boy, Daniel followed Sam down the slippery bank and along the narrow strip of rocky ground that edged the river.

Daniel watched helplessly as the rushing water swirled around Charity and Henry. He felt frozen in place as suddenly the memory of that terrifying April night two years ago flashed through his mind. The deafening explosion. The other-worldly sense of being hurled from the hurricane deck of the *Sultana* as if shot from a cannon. Plunging into the dark, swirling, muddy currents of the Mississippi. His lungs burning while he frantically fought to reach the surface of the river, unable to discern what was up and what was down. Breaking through to the surface and pulling life-giving air into his lungs, while the sounds of hundreds of men dying around him filled his ears.

Although the temperature had undoubtedly dipped below freezing, beads of sweat broke out on Daniel's forehead. For nearly two years, his fear of drowning had exceeded even what he'd felt at his baptism of fire on the battlefield. He had a vague sense of Sam beside him, shucking off his boots and coat and wading into the neck-high water.

A sharp cracking sound split the air, followed by Charity's screams. The limb she was holding onto had broken, sending her sluicing farther down the stream and leaving Henry clinging alone to the fallen tree.

Charity's arms reached up, thrashing wildly at the fast-moving water. Her intermittent screams turned to desperate garbled wails. Twice, her head went completely beneath the surface.

Charity was drowning.

Daniel's body jerked with a mighty shudder as if he'd been struck by lightning. A fear, far greater than any he'd ever experienced, shot through him, thawing his frozen limbs. With his gaze fastened on Charity's flailing figure, he ripped off his boots and coat and strode into the cold river.

Dear Lord, just give me the strength to save them.

seventeen

Gasping for air, Charity struggled to stand as she fought against the frigid current that dragged her down while pushing her westward. But her left leg buckled, refusing to support her. When she slid down the steep bank after Henry, her leg had smacked into a large rock just as she went into the river. She vaguely remembered hearing a sickening *crunch* and *snap* as a searing pain shot up her lower leg to her hip. But the icy water had quickly washed away the pain, and her mind, focused on wrenching Henry from the lethal clutches of the Muscatatuck, had ignored her injury.

Her only thought had been to hold onto Henry, keeping his head above the roiling water that was shoving them both downstream. Blessedly, as she and the boy slid past a fallen tree, she'd managed to grab a limb and hold them fast, while alternately screaming for both Daniel and Sam.

But amid her prayers for deliverance and her cries for help, the branch that had been her and Henry's lifeline snapped. At the same time, she'd lost her grip on Henry.

Henry. She couldn't see Henry! An overwhelming sense of grief and panic seized her. Then out of the corner of her eye, she saw Sam towing Henry toward a snow-covered sandbar—a tiny icy island jutting up from the center of the river.

Thank You, Jesus!

But her relief gave way to a new terror. Glancing at the shore, she saw Daniel wade into the river only to be knocked off his feet by the strong current. He immediately disappeared beneath the river's surface. She tried to scream his name, but her throat refused to make a sound.

A silent sob tore from deep inside her. Her arms that burned with exhaustion felt leaden, sapped of their last ounce of strength. With Daniel gone, the will to fight left her.

When she'd learned of Granger's death, she'd cried. Yet that grief had not extinguished the life-spark within her. But now that the Muscatatuck had taken Daniel, she was content to let the river take her, too. With one last, sweet gulp of air, she stopped fighting to keep her face above the rushing water and slipped beneath it.

Suddenly, an iron-tight grip around her chest propelled her upwards, into the winter gloaming and life-giving air. How had Sam, in such a short amount of time, managed to get Henry to the sandbar and still get back to help her?

But when she cocked her head, she saw that her rescuer had jet-black—not sandy-colored—hair.

Daniel!

Thank You Jesus, thank You! Her silent prayer winged its way heavenward as she rested against him.

When they reached the riverbank, he helped her to her feet. But blinding pain exploded in her left leg, and it collapsed under her.

She felt her body being lifted in Daniel's strong arms then gently lowered to the snow. She wanted to tell him how glad she was that he was alive. But her eyes kept closing and her mouth wouldn't open. Icy numbness gripped her.

A flurry of commotion swirled around them. Many voices. People running. Shouting.

Daniel's quick, warm breaths caressed her face. His hands shook as he wrapped her in his wool coat, ordered someone to make sure she didn't fall asleep, and then headed back into the river.

"Daniel! Daniel!" Sobs convulsed from her shivering body.

"Shh, shh, ma chère, you are safe. You will be all right," Annie Martin's voice soothed. The old woman crouched beside Charity in the snow, rocking her in slender, wiry arms. "It is a good thing you have strong lungs, hey? I reckon everyone along East Jackson Street heard you hollerin'."

Charity could only repeat Daniel's name. Why had he left her? Why had he gone back?

A cacophony of voices around her barraged her frozen brain. The only thing she heard clearly was an unidentifiable voice saying, "They found him. He's drowned."

A mind-numbing, spirit-crippling anguish gripped Charity. Her last conscious thought was that Annie was wrong. Daniel was gone, and she would never be all right again. Then a blessed blackness engulfed her.

❧

Charity's first sensation was one of warmth as she struggled to emerge from the dense fog shrouding her mind. Next, she noticed a dull, throbbing pain in her left leg. A low moan sounded, and somehow she realized it had come from her own throat.

She rolled her head on the soft, down pillow, inhaling the familiar scent. She was home. Aunt Jennie had all of her bed linens washed in lemon-verbena-scented lye soap.

Although her lips felt thick and numb, she strained to enunciate the beloved name screaming through her heart. "Daniel."

"I'm sorry, Charity. He's gone." Aunt Jennie's soft voice hovered above Charity. Her words sent a new wave of crushing sadness rolling through Charity's chest. Tears stung her eyes then slipped from their corners to course down her cheeks to her neck. How she wished she'd told him that she loved him.

Aunt Jennie patted Charity's hand. "Now, now, dear. He will be back soon."

Charity blinked at her aunt's astounding statement. What could she mean?

"He went to the railroad depot to telegraph his father. He insists we allow Dr. Morgan to attend you," Aunt Jennie said, answering Charity's bewildered gaze. "I told him he should rest after such an awful ordeal, but he insisted—"

"Daniel's alive?" Unspeakable joy burst like Fourth of July fireworks inside Charity. *Thank You, Jesus! Thank You, thank You.* Then she suddenly remembered the words someone had muttered on the riverbank. "He's drowned."

The image of Henry bobbing in the icy river appeared before her mind's eye. She'd seen Sam put Henry on the sandbar. Could the child have slipped back into the river?

"Henry!" Frantic, she tried to push up with her elbow.

Aunt Jennie gently pressed her shoulders back against the pillow. "Henry is fine. He's asleep in the spare room down the hall."

"But someone said—they said. . . ." Charity had to force the grim words from her lips. "Someone said, 'He's drowned.'"

Aunt Jennie made soft tsking sounds as she tucked the wool blankets and quilt snugly beneath Charity's chin. "I'm sorry to have to tell you, Charity, but Mr. Porter perished."

"Sam?" A jumble of emotions Charity didn't have the strength to untangle balled up inside her.

Sadness laced Aunt Jennie's somber tone. "Daniel said that when he went to rescue you, he saw Mr. Porter put Henry on a sandbar. He assumed both father and son had made it to safety. But when he got back to Henry, Sam was gone." Both her voice and her gaze lowered. "They found Sam's body about a half mile downstream."

Aunt Jennie glanced through the open doorway to the short hall, sniffed, and pulled a handkerchief from her sleeve to dab at her nose and eyes. "Poor little Henry. Poor little orphaned mite. Had to watch his own papa drown." She shook her head and dabbed at her eyes again.

Although sad to learn of Sam's tragic death, Charity was consoled by the knowledge that Henry was well and safe—at last. However harsh Sam's previous treatment of his son, he'd died heroically, sacrificing his life for his child's. At least Henry's last memory of his father would be a positive one.

Charity shifted in bed, and the throbbing pain in her leg increased, causing her to moan.

Immediately attentive, Aunt Jennie fussed with Charity's pillow and covers. "I'm sorry, dear, but it's too soon to give you more of the laudanum Dr. Grayson left."

Another puzzle. Charity groaned, wishing her mind didn't feel so foggy, as if in a perpetual state of half-sleep. If their family physician, Dr. Grayson, had already attended her, why would Daniel feel it necessary to call his father to come all the way from Madison?

"Aunt Jennie, if Dr. Grayson has been here and seen to my injuries, why did Daniel go. . . ?"

A stricken look creased Aunt Jennie's forehead and she twisted the handkerchief in her hands. "Charity, dear, I'm afraid your leg is terribly, terribly broken." Her throat moved with a hard swallow, and her gaze slid to her lap. "Dr. Grayson suggested an extreme procedure to which Daniel violently objected."

A new alarm brought Charity's head up from the pillow. "Aunt Jennie, tell me plainly. What did Dr. Grayson suggest?"

"Amputation." The word left Aunt Jennie's lips on a quavering breath.

Charity sank back against the pillow. A blessed numbness gripped her, not unlike what she'd felt while in the Muscatatuck River. What if Dr. Morgan came to the same conclusion? What kind of altered life lay ahead for her?

Sam Porter had lost his life. She felt almost ashamed to grieve the potential loss of a limb. But she'd seen the pity in the eyes of many who looked upon war amputees. Perhaps she, too, had cast pitying looks at those unfortunates.

Aunt Jennie's head bowed as she squeezed Charity's hand. She'd gone to Christ in prayer.

She followed her aunt's example. But her prayer was not one of self-pity but praise. Daniel was alive!

Her leg might be irreparably damaged, but her heart lightly

skipped in her chest. Even in her semiconscious state, the spark of life that had sputtered and gone out inside her when she thought Daniel had died flamed anew. Any lingering doubt that she loved him had been extinguished tonight in the icy Muscatatuck River.

Sleep dragged at her eyelids, and she could feel consciousness slipping away. As she struggled to fashion a coherent prayer, she found little room for self-pity.

Dear Heavenly Father, I pray that You will allow me to keep my leg. But if not, give me the strength to face what's before me. Grant Sam mercy and comfort Henry. And thank You for saving Daniel. Just take care of Daniel.

"Daniel. Daniel. . . ."

She drifted off to sleep with the sweet taste of Daniel's name on her lips.

eighteen

"Charity. Charity, are you awake?" The voice sounded distant, as if she was at the bottom of a well and someone was at the top, calling down to her.

She squinted, struggling to open her eyes fully. But the glare from the window stabbed painfully at her eyes until a large form moved, blocking it.

"Are you in much pain, my dear?" When the face first came into her field of vision, she thought it was Daniel's. But then she noticed the streaks of gray in the older man's black hair. Dr. Morgan's dark eyes were full of concern as they peered into hers.

The morning's events pieced themselves together like a crazy quilt in Charity's mind. She remembered Dr. Morgan walking into her room and examining her injured leg, his expression guarded. The last she recalled was Aunt Jennie holding her hand and praying over her while Dr. Morgan pressed an ether-laced cloth to her mouth.

"Only a little," she mumbled. The sunlight streaming through her window told her it was early afternoon. Her insides shuddered at the thought of what might have transpired while she was unconscious. But she had to know.

"Is it. . ." Charity couldn't bring herself to say the word "gone." She was well aware that the sharp, stinging pain assailing her lower leg offered no assurance that she'd kept the limb. During the war, she'd helped nurse wounded soldiers when her church served as a makeshift hospital. Many times, those who'd lost limbs remarked that they still felt pain in a leg that was no longer there.

Dr. Morgan moved the covers to expose her left side.

She hitched up her courage and looked down at the place where her limb should be. A dizzying wave of relief rolled through her. Wrapped tightly in white bandages, her leg—still attached to her body—was encased in a wire and wood apparatus that protruded beyond her nightdress.

"I must admit yours was a complicated injury, and setting the bones was a real challenge. Both the tibia and the fibula are broken, and the fibula—the small bone in your leg—is broken in a couple of places. I don't fault Dr. Grayson. Amputation would have been the simpler and arguably safer choice of treatment." He shook his head. "But at your age, I felt it was worth trying to save the limb if at all possible. I managed to set the bones, and with proper care, I believe there is a very good chance that you will regain full use of the leg." Dr. Morgan's kind smile helped to further ease her anxiety. "I have it wrapped and fitted with a Hodgen wire cradle extension splint. The apparatus will exert the right amount of pull on the muscles so they won't draw up, shortening the leg as the bones heal."

He gently draped the quilt back over her injured leg. "If diligently attended, your leg should heal soundly in a couple of months. About the time the first crocuses bloom," he added with a grin.

"Where's Daniel?" Charity was aghast that the question traipsing about the confines of her mind had escaped her lips. The fact that Daniel had refrained from visiting her since he'd pulled her from the river pinched her heart painfully.

Dr. Morgan smiled fondly. "He's asleep—for the first time in over twenty-four hours from what I understand."

The doctor shook his head. "I still find it hard to believe he entered that river twice of his own volition. Since nearly drowning when the steamboat, *Sultana*, sank, I haven't known him to so much as dip a toe into any substantial body of water."

"Daniel was on the *Sultana*?" Charity felt her eyes widen. She remembered reading in the spring of '65, the horrifying account in the local newspaper, the *Plain Dealer*. Most who'd lost their lives in the disaster were Union soldiers returning from the war. Although a Southerner, she recalled thinking how awful it must have been for the victims' families to learn that their loved ones made it through the war only to die in a steamboat explosion on their way home. The full recognition of Daniel's courage yesterday struck her a reeling blow.

Dr. Morgan nodded as he carefully straightened the covers back over her leg. "Thankfully, he was thrown clear of the boat and didn't suffer the burns experienced by most of the survivors of the calamity. But I think nearly drowning in the Mississippi River scared him more than anything he experienced during the war—including the time he spent in Andersonville."

Charity lay stunned, trying to assimilate what she'd just learned. Even among Southerners, the name of the infamous prisoner-of-war camp at Andersonville, Georgia, was often whispered in shame, so hideous were the stories that came out of that place. That Daniel had endured both the horrors of that awful camp and the terror of the *Sultana* disaster was almost beyond comprehension.

She turned a helpless look to Dr. Morgan. What could she say as a Southerner? But as upon her previous visits to his home, she found no guile in his kind face. A Christian in the truest sense, it appeared Dr. Ephraim Morgan's only enemies were the myriad physical ills that afflicted God's children.

The doctor bent to retrieve his medical bag from the floor. When he straightened, he fixed her with a serious, knowing look. "Miss Langdon," he said quietly, "I've never questioned my son's courage or inherent goodness, but it took a very strong emotion—stronger than those I've mentioned—to propel him into that river."

Charity's heart thudded painfully in her chest. Was he trying to tell her Daniel cared for her—loved her?

He plucked his hat from a hook on the wall, plopped it on his head, and gave it a quick tap. His smile—that reminded her so much of Daniel's—returned.

"Weather permitting, I shall come weekly to check on your progress. I'll have your aunt send up a light meal, perhaps some good, rich chicken broth and bread, to help knit those bones back together. Beyond that, I prescribe rest."

"Thank you, Dr. Morgan." The words seemed inadequate for someone who had just saved her leg. Charity's lashes beat back stinging tears and she gave him a faint, parting nod, although she doubted she could eat anything. The lingering taste of ether in her mouth had robbed her appetite and left her nauseous.

Heaving a sigh, she listened to the doctor's footfalls fade down the stairs and clamped her lips tight together. As for his instruction to rest, it seemed she had little choice in the matter. She'd never been one to loll about, and the thought of being confined to bed for two months felt like a prison sentence.

That thought reminded her of what Dr. Morgan had shared about Daniel. The notion that Daniel could care for her—a Southerner—after being incarcerated in Andersonville was overwhelming.

New tears slipped hotly from the corners of her eyes to puddle in her ears. She remembered Daniel's kiss at Lucy's engagement party and how she had pulled away from his embrace. She rolled her head on the pillow until her mother's picture, encased in the frame Daniel had made for it, came into view.

The groan that welled up from the depths of her insides did not reflect the pain in her leg. Regret pressed like a stone on her chest. For months, Daniel had reached out to her. Yet time and again, she'd responded by rebuffing his attentions. And then he'd faced his worst fear to save her.

Charity stretched out her hand, trying to touch the picture frame Daniel's hands had fashioned. But it sat just beyond her reach. With a sigh, she sank back against her pillow, allowing her arm to fall across her chest. Forlornness draped heavily around her spirit. Was Daniel, too, just beyond her reach now?

Why hadn't he come to see her? Had she squandered the last drop of his goodwill?

Charity welcomed the encroaching slumber tugging heavily on her eyelids. But before the last bit of consciousness seeped away, she whispered one plea to the darkening room.

"Dear Lord, let Dr. Morgan be right. Let Daniel love me."

nineteen

"You're bound 'n' determined to give that Dr. Morgan a conniption fit, ain't ya?"

From her perch on the bed, Charity looked up to see Pearl march into the room. The girl's brown face was pruned up in a scowl that foretold a scolding as she plopped a bundle of letters on the bed beside Charity.

"The biznus mail," Pearl said unnecessarily.

To help fill Charity's long days, Uncle Silas had begun having Pearl pick up the mail from the post office each day and have Charity sort through it, separating the bills from other correspondence.

Charity gave the bundle of envelopes tied with a string a cursory glance and grunted in answer. She continued to ease her leg encased in the cumbersome Hodgen splint over the side of the bed. It had taken her a full ten minutes to untie the sandbag weights that normally kept a constant tension on her foot.

Pearl crossed her arms over her chest and glared at Charity. "Do you wanna limp fer the rest o' yer life? Dr. Morgan said them weights'll keep the muscles in yer leg from drawin' up so yer leg won't heal shorter'n it oughta be."

Undaunted, Charity allowed gravity to drag her limb imprisoned in the heavy metal brace over the side of the bed. "Surely takin' the weights off for a few minutes won't do any harm, Pearl. I just get so terribly tired of lyin' in that one position."

Though thrilled her friend had come to nurse her, Charity sometimes wished Pearl didn't take her job so seriously. It still made her smile to remember how two days after the accident, Pearl strode into the sickroom with all the authority of an army field general and declared, "Ain't gonna let nobody see to ya 'cept me an' Dr. Morgan. 'Specially not that sawbones that wanted to lop off yer leg!"

With Pearl's help, Charity maneuvered herself into a sitting position on the edge of her bed. She wiggled her bare toes sticking out from the wire cage–like restraint. Tingles pricked at her foot as the blood rushed into it, and she grimaced. But even a few minutes of respite from lying on her back would feel good.

Crouching beside her, Pearl carefully arranged Charity's cotton skirt to completely cover her bare legs.

"School'll be out in a few minutes, so young master Henry'll be along d'rectly. Got to git you decent." Finishing her task, Pearl rose and flashed a fond smile. "You know that chil' don't knock, holler, nor nothin'. Jist rushes in here like a cat with his tail afire!"

Charity chortled at Pearl's accurate description. She thanked the Lord for Henry's childlike resiliency. The week following his father's funeral he'd seemed sad and withdrawn. But then the grief lifted like a somber fog, and Henry emerged his former cheerful self. Yet he still talked of his desire to return to Georgia.

Charity had no idea if the boy still had relatives there. And even if he did, she didn't have the first notion how she might go about locating them. But she understood Henry's desire to return to his native state—a desire she shared. But lately she'd begun feeling a tug to stay in Indiana. And she knew why.

Daniel.

As if reading her mind, Pearl shot Charity a teasing grin over her shoulder before crossing the room to her sewing chair. "An' Henry ain't the only feller comin'. You *know* Mr. Morgan'll be along, jist as sure as I'm sittin' here," she said, plopping herself into the chair.

Warmth infused Charity's cheeks. To cover her blush, she turned and reached for the bundle of envelopes beside her. Thankfully, Daniel had quickly banished her worries that he wanted nothing more to do with her. In fact, he'd proved a faithful visitor, daily bringing by the mill receipts and discussing everything from the price of grain to the subject of Reverend Davenport's latest sermon.

Although she had thanked Daniel repeatedly for saving her and Henry from drowning, she never mentioned what his father had told her about Andersonville or the *Sultana*. It had seemed a gift from God that Daniel still wished to spend time with her. She'd lacked the courage to mention anything that might tarnish their relationship that grew increasingly closer and warmer. Indeed, as the winter days passed, fusing her broken bones, Charity realized they were also fusing her heart—her spirit—with Daniel's.

She looked over at Pearl working on a piece of tatting that would decorate her wedding dress. Guilt rasped against Charity's conscience. In a few weeks, Pearl would be getting married. She should be in Madison, working on her wedding dress with Tunia and helping to fix up the house in Georgetown Andrew bought for them.

"I'm sorry, Pearl." Charity gazed at her friend who sat humming a hymn as she focused on the work in her hands. "You shouldn't be here. You should be in Madison, gettin' things ready for your weddin'. In fact, I'm doin' fine. You really don't need to stay—"

"'Course I need to stay!" Pearl's face yanked up, but her stern look quickly dissolved into an appreciative smile.

"Mammy says I'll do Adam good to miss me some 'fore the weddin'. 'Sides, I git a letter from him pert-near every day." She dropped her gaze back to her needlework, but not before Charity noticed a telltale glistening in her friend's dark eyes that sent new thorns of guilt pricking at her conscience.

Charity undid the string Postmaster McClelland had tied around the handful of envelopes. Pearl was right. She would have little time to complete her task before Henry arrived. She reached for a pencil on the bedside table to mark each missive according to its contents.

Suddenly her hand froze. The first envelope in the stack had originally been addressed to Sam Porter, but the postmaster had marked through his name and written "The Gants" above it.

The return address in the upper left corner read, "New South Investors, Atlanta, Georgia." It was the same name and address she'd seen on the pamphlet Sam had shown her at Christmas. This was probably a reply to Sam's inquiry about Southern land for sale. A letter would need to be sent to the company informing them of Sam's tragic death. And since Uncle Silas disliked writing letters, Charity had no doubt the errand would fall to her.

She broke the envelope's seal with her thumb and slipped out the single sheet of folded paper. As she perused the letter, her heart thumped harder and her eyes widened. It offered, for five dollars per acre, land in her home county of Fulton, Georgia, along Peachtree Creek. It was signed, "Armand Dubois, Esquire, New South Investors."

Charity had no doubt the man was a carpetbagger. But the notion that land near her childhood home could be obtained so cheaply tempted her imagination. Also, if Mr. Dubois was acquainted with the area, he might be able to help her discover whether Henry still had relatives in or near Fulton County. Sam's words echoed tantalizingly in her ears. *"We could go back—you, me, and Henry. We could start anew."*

Pearl eyed Charity over her needlework. "Sump'un wrong? You look like you done seen a ghost!"

Charity ran her tongue over her dry lips as she quickly folded the paper and tucked it back into the envelope. Something restrained her from divulging to Pearl all of her thoughts on what she'd just read. "Just carpetbaggers tryin' to sell Georgia land to Sam," Charity said, trying to sound unaffected even as tempting possibilities swirled through her mind. The moment she left Georgian soil nearly two and a half years ago, Charity had vowed to return. During her time here in Vernon, she'd saved nearly a hundred dollars from both her job at the mill and her wages teaching school, hoping to one day use it to return to Fulton County and try to reclaim her parent's land.

At the quick, staccato-like sound of Henry's footsteps running up the stairs, Charity jerked. She hurriedly slid the letter beneath the stack of other envelopes, which she moved to the table beside her bed. If Henry happened to see his father's name on the envelope, it might rekindle the boy's grief.

"Miss Charity!" Henry blew through the open doorway like a miniature whirlwind. His enthusiastic hug nearly knocked her sideways on the bed.

He unceremoniously dropped his schoolbooks held together by a leather belt beside her on the quilt top.

"Daniel let me ride home in his wagon," he said breathlessly. "He said I could help at the mill this Saturday if Uncle Silas says it's all right. Do you think Uncle Silas will say it's all right?"

In his exuberance, Henry bumped against her metal splint. "I'm sorry. I didn't mean to hurt your leg. When will your leg get out of the cage anyway? Daniel says he misses you at the mill. Are you going to go back to work at the mill or are you going to be our teacher again?"

Charity laughed at Henry's barrage of questions, but a squiggle of joy shot through her learning Daniel missed seeing her at the mill.

"You didn't hurt my leg, Henry. And let's take one question at a time." She brushed back the shock of sandy hair falling across Henry's forehead. "You'll have to ask Uncle Silas. But if you promise not to make a nuisance of yourself, I imagine he will allow you to help at the mill. And," she added, "you must get all the lessons done Miss Gannon has assigned to you." After her accident, Charity had worried that her students would be left without a teacher. So she'd been greatly relieved to learn that a soon-to-be-graduated student of the normal school had taken over her teaching duties.

"I will." He fiddled with the loose end of the belt that girdled his books. "But if I learn how to work in a mill, I can work in one when I go back to live in Georgia."

Charity shared a concerned glance with Pearl. A day never passed that Henry didn't remind them he wished to one day return to Georgia. It made the thought-provoking letter from New South Investors even more enticing.

"So when are you gettin' the cage off your leg?" Childlike, Henry reiterated his earlier question. "'Cause Daniel made you crut—" He clapped his hand over his mouth just as Daniel appeared, filling the open doorway.

"You little scamp! You let the cat out of the bag, didn't you?" Daniel's good-natured laughter sent a thrill rippling through Charity.

With a quick greeting to both Charity and Pearl, a grinning Daniel brought from behind him two oak crutches, the tops of which were padded with a bright blue and yellow calico print.

Henry hopped down from the bed and bounded to Daniel like an eager pup. "Miss Charity says she thinks Uncle Silas will let me help you at the mill."

Daniel gave Henry a fond smile, and it struck Charity how easy it would be to imagine the three of them making a little family.

"Well, he's downstairs. Why don't you go ask him?" Daniel tousled Henry's hair as the boy rushed past him, out of the door, and down the stairs.

Daniel stepped into the room and held the crutches out for Charity's inspection.

"Thank you, Daniel." Charity pushed the words past the lump in her throat. This was the second time she'd benefited from his excellent handiwork.

He leaned the crutches against the wall beside her bed. "When Pa takes that iron thing off your leg, I'll help you learn to walk with them."

Smiling, Charity nodded. But her smile faded when her gaze slid from the crutches against the wall to the stack of envelopes on the bedside table, reminding her of Mr. Dubois' offer.

She looked at Daniel's handsome face stretched in a sweet smile and winced inwardly from the pain of having her heart tugged hard in opposite directions.

twenty

Charity glanced for the umpteenth time at the clock above the mantel. It was not like Daniel to be a half hour late.

Needing to do something, she reached for the crutches propped against the wall beside her bed. Three weeks ago, Dr. Morgan had removed the cumbersome Hodgen splint, replacing it with a more ambulatory set of splints. Since then, she'd been practicing maneuvering around her room with the help of the crutches Daniel had fashioned for her.

She shoved the cotton and calico padded tops of the crutches under her arms and hobbled to the window.

"Quit yer frettin'. He's comin'. Don't he always come?" A teasing giggle rippled through Pearl's chide. Seated in the wingback chair beside the fireplace, she grinned up from the knitting in her hands.

Yes, he always did come. Charity gazed down on Perry Street as if she might make him appear. When, she wondered, had Daniel's daily visits become as vital to her as the air she breathed?

Suddenly, she noticed the halting, uneven footfalls on the staircase—a sound now dear to her. Her heart thumped harder and she turned from the window.

"See, I told ya." Shooting Charity a smug grin, Pearl gathered up her knitting, plopped it in the basket beside her chair, and headed for the door.

"Where are you goin'?" Charity swung her crutches out in front of her and planted them solidly on the carpet, propelling herself forward. Never once had Pearl left her unchaperoned.

"I have to help Mrs. Akers with somethin' in the kitchen," Pearl mumbled the vague excuse on her way out of the room, nodding at Daniel on his way in. "Afternoon, Mr. Morgan."

The sly grin Pearl shot Charity over her shoulder irked her. Charity knew Pearl Emanuel too well not to know when she was up to something.

"I'm sorry I'm late." Even in his dark wool work shirt and trousers, he looked so handsome that, as Lucy had once said about Travis, it made her eyes hurt.

An odd, almost caressing look in his eyes sent Charity's heart pounding painfully against her ribs. How embarrassing if he should guess she'd worried he might not come.

"Why Daniel, is it past time for your usual visit? I hadn't noticed," she drawled in her best, slightly bored Southern-lady voice.

Attempting to hide the blush she felt flaring in her cheeks, she turned quickly away from him on her crutches. But with her abrupt movement, the tip of one crutch caught in the rug and she pitched forward with a decidedly unladylike yelp.

About the time she expected her face to smack the carpet, it was cradled instead against the soft wool of Daniel's shirt. She could feel the low rumble of his laugh bubble up inside him before it burst forth.

"Oh, Charity. You really shouldn't try to lie. You are so terrible at it."

He turned her gently in his strong embrace until she faced him. Neither spoke as he drew her closer, their locked gazes uttering in unison the soundless sentiments of their hearts.

Resting in the secure circle of his arms, she tipped her head back, closed her eyes, and welcomed his kiss. This time, she didn't pull away. No ugly specters from the past popped up to spoil her joy. This was Daniel. No one else. Good, sweet, beloved Daniel. The man who owned her every heartbeat. The man she loved.

"Sweetheart," he whispered warmly against her hair. "I was late because I have some very important things to discuss with you, and I wanted to rehearse them so I'd say them just right."

He gently helped her over to the edge of bed then pulled up a chair so he could face her. "Charity, you have become exceedingly dear to me," he began. Leaning forward, he took her hands into his and shook his head. "No. More than dear. Beloved."

He paused, and the tip of his tongue peeked out to moisten his lips or perhaps taste the lingering remnants of their kiss. "The day I walked into your uncle's sawmill I found a job, but I lost my heart. I've known for months that you are the woman I want by my side for the rest of my life."

His gaze dropped to their linked hands. "For the past several weeks I feel we've grown even closer. That the past—things that once might have been impediments to our mutual happiness—no longer matters—"

"Daniel." Amid the cacophony of the wild, joyful celebration his words triggered inside her, a small, rasping voice of foreboding slinked out to squelch her bliss. The war might be over, the past behind them; but just since her accident she'd learned things about Daniel she hadn't known. About the *Sultana*—and Andersonville. She couldn't bear the thought of worrying each day of their lives that some obscure memory might suddenly emerge, souring their sweet love.

She gave his fingers a gentle squeeze and fixed him with an unflinching gaze. As tempting as it was to lightly dismiss the fact that they'd been on opposite sides of the war, she couldn't risk it. "Your father told me you were in Andersonville."

Daniel paled slightly. "That was in the past. It doesn't have any bearing on—"

"It might." She shook her head and prayed for courage. They had to get it all out—everything. They had to get past this. "Daniel, we need to talk about it. All of it. We can't just pretend it didn't happen, shove it back until one day it's grown into a monster that pounces from its hidin' place to rip our love to shreds."

His body heaved with a mighty sigh, and he shook his head

somberly. The muscles working in his angled jaw spoke of his dread.

Charity screwed up her courage and began. "Andersonville. I heard it was—"

"Yes. It was. Everything you heard and more." An anger, so intense it frightened her, flickered in his dark eyes.

"Tell me. Tell me all of it." Charity stiffened her back and prayed God would give her the courage to bear all she was about to learn.

Daniel drew in and blew out a deep breath, scoured his face with his unsteady hand, then obliged her request. Over the space of an excruciating half hour, he shared with her the horrors to which her countrymen had subjected him and many of his compatriots.

She learned how a guard had broken his leg with an iron bar when he'd attempted to intervene in the beatings of two of his friends. She wept as he described how he'd had to set his own leg, making a splint from the broken lengths of a lean-to pole. By the time he finished with the frightening recounting of the *Sultana* tragedy, Charity's cheeks were drenched.

"I'm sorry. I'm so sorry." The words sounded woefully inadequate.

At last, a gut-wrenching breath shuddered through Daniel as if he were expelling the last of his demons. His features looked weary—drained of energy. But the angry flame in his eyes had been quenched. "Your turn," he murmured with a nod, his expression somber.

Charity felt spent. As bad as her experiences had been, they didn't compare to what he'd described. But just as she needed to know of his sufferings, he needed to know of hers.

She hugged herself to still her shaking body and tried to determine where to start. "Papa died of dropsy just as the war broke out. Asa was seventeen and itchin' to join the Confederate Army. But havin' just lost Papa, Mamma forbad it. She told Asa he had to stay and help run the cotton mill." Charity grimaced, remembering the terrible argument between her mother and brother. "But Asa had no interest in millin' cotton, and it was really Jericho and I who ran the mill."

Daniel nodded. The concerned interest on his face encouraged her to continue.

Charity blew out a frayed breath then forged on. "Mamma never got over losin' Papa. Her health failed, and a year later she succumbed to lung fever." She paused to get a better grip on her emotions, focusing on her hands wringing in her lap. If she looked at Daniel now, she'd fling herself into his arms and sob. "The day after Mamma's funeral, Asa joined the army."

Daniel reached out and clasped her hands warmly in his. "And you never saw your brother again?"

Charity sniffed and forced a smile, remembering her last conversation with her brother. "I saw him once more, briefly. It was July 19, 1864. The day before he died."

Daniel let go of her hands and an odd look crossed his face. Taking his action as a cue to resume her narrative, Charity continued. "Asa stopped by the house to tell me he was camped less than a mile away with General Hood's army." Charity's words tumbled out more quickly as she remembered her frantic attempt to keep her brother safe. "I told him I feared there'd be a battle, because I'd just come from the creek and had spied three Union soldiers there fillin' their canteens. Asa kissed my cheek then took off like the devil was after him. That was the last time. . . ."

Charity suddenly sensed an odd tenseness in Daniel. An ominous stillness fell between them like the foreboding quiet before a storm. She looked at his face that had gone chalk-white.

He rose slowly. Deliberately. Without a word, he simply turned and walked out of the door.

Charity sat stunned and bewildered, listening to his familiar halting steps descending the stairs. What on earth could she have said that would have caused him to react so?

"Daniel." His name came out in a pitiful croak when she

finally found her voice.

The sound of his steps paused for an instant then resumed, finally fading away.

Charity sat as if paralyzed, a terrible dread gripping her chest like an icy fist. Although she couldn't begin to guess why, she knew with excruciating certainty that Daniel Morgan would not be back.

twenty-one

"I won't allow it."

Lying on his back in bed, Daniel stiffened at his mother's voice. Why couldn't everyone just leave him be? Was a little solitude too much to ask?

The bed creaked in protest as he slowly pushed himself to a sitting position on the quilt top and swung his legs over the side. He strove to shove down the resentment rising inside him. In his twenty-seven years of life, he'd never shown disrespect to his mother, and he wouldn't start now.

Daniel heaved a sigh and looked up at his mother's resolute figure in the doorway. "Won't allow what, Mother?" he asked in a leaden tone.

"You know very well what!" She planted her fists atop her hips on either side of her still-trim waist. The all too familiar signal that he was in for an extended siege evoked an inward groan from Daniel.

Mother stepped across the threshold into his room. "I won't allow you to cloister yourself away day after day—"

"Three days, Mother. I've only been back home for three days." His words that seemed not to faze his mother struck Daniel full force. It felt like three lifetimes since he'd learned that Charity—the woman who'd won his heart—had been responsible for his and his men's capture.

Mother took another step closer. "What is going on, Daniel? You simply appear at the house, say only that you've quit your job at the mill in Vernon, and closet yourself up here like a recluse. You don't eat. Don't sleep. Oh yes," she answered his surprised glance, "we hear you pacing your room, tromping up and down the stairs at all hours—"

"Is there something you require of me, Mother?" Daniel sprang to his feet and strode to the window. If activity would bring an end to his mother's and Lucy's constant nagging, he'd happily chop firewood for the whole of Madison! "If there is something you would like for me to do for you, I'd be glad to do it."

Mother's weary sigh gouged at Daniel's heart. Her voice softened, which was so much harder to bear than her earlier scolding tone. "Yes, Daniel. I need—we all need—to know what happened. Why you left Vernon. Daniel, whatever it is that's troubling you, you shouldn't let it fester."

Stifling a sardonic snort, Daniel stuffed his hands into his pockets and looked out of the window, seeing nothing. He'd never understood the notion that laying a wounded heart open, exposing its injuries to the harsh light of day, somehow promoted healing. Even animals knew enough to crawl off to a dark, secluded place to lick their wounds.

"Does it have to do with Miss Langdon?" Mother's gentle, coaxing voice did nothing to relax Daniel's shoulder muscles that tensed at her touch. "Because if it does, you recovered from Phoebe's rejection and you shall recover ̶ "

"Yes, Mother, it has to do with Charity!" Daniel whirled to face her. His mother's words had finally managed to lance the festering sore on his heart. So she must deal with the ugliness her determination had freed. "It has to do with Charity. . .and me and Fred and Tom!"

At her puzzled look, he recounted what Charity had told him. At last, Daniel fashioned into words the hideous truth that had haunted his brain like a shapeless, dark apparition these past three days. "It was Charity who put me, Fred, and Tom in Andersonville. I limp because of Charity. Fred and Tom are dead because of Charity."

Only the long silence that stretched between them indicated his mother's shocked surprise. But in truth, he never expected his stunning revelation to evoke any outward sign of dismay from his unflappable parent. Years of training her countenance to remain serene before seriously ill patients had given his mother a poker face to rival that of the most skilled gambler.

"My darling, it was the war. I'm sure she had no idea the consequences of telling her brother that she'd seen the three of you."

His mother's sweet smile made Daniel want to bury his head in her shoulder and sob as he did when he was young. But he wouldn't allow her—or anyone—to manufacture excuses for Charity's actions.

"What difference does it make why she did it, Mother?" Daniel rubbed his forehead. "The fact is she did it."

"And what was her response when you told her you were among the men captured?"

Daniel turned back to the window. This was the question he'd most dreaded. His abrupt departure—that he'd simply walked away from Charity—had bothered him since he left Vernon. "I didn't tell her. I just left."

"Oh, Daniel." The disappointment in Mother's voice stung worse than if she'd slapped him. He knew his parents prided themselves in having raised him and Lucy with exemplary manners.

He turned and forced himself to meet his mother's look of dismay, his gaze pleading for understanding. "I couldn't stay in that room, Mother. Not another moment. Not after I learned that two of the best friends I've ever had—men who saved my life more times than I care to count—lay dead because of the woman I. . . ." He couldn't bring himself to finish the thought.

"The woman you love?" Mother softly finished it for him.

Daniel nodded, not trusting his voice.

After a long pause during which Daniel assumed she was weighing her next words, Mother blew out another soft sigh. "Have you asked God's guidance in this?"

This time, Daniel didn't even try to stifle his sarcastic snort.

"Why would I ask God for guidance when He allowed me to fall in love with the woman who has the blood of my friends on her hands?" He rubbed his hand across his forehead so hard it hurt.

"You'll never rub it away, you know." Mother's voice had taken on a hard edge. "Ever since you returned from the war, you've been rubbing your head like you're trying to rub away the images there. You won't talk to your father, or me, or even Lucy about what happened to you. And you won't let us talk about it."

She folded her arms over her chest and cocked her head. A small smile tipped up her lips. "Do you remember the time when Lucy was little and I asked her to sweep dirt from the parlor carpet?"

Daniel couldn't imagine how that incident—one of Lucy's many childish acts of mischief—could have anything to do with his current situation. But eager to steer the conversation in another direction, he nodded. "You praised her for doing a good job of it and even gave her a penny and had me take her down to the drug store to buy a stick of candy." He chuckled at the memory, in spite of himself. "Come to find out, the little swindler had swept the carpet all right but had hid all the dirt under it."

"That's you, Daniel." Mother's gaze bored into him. "The hate you still carry in your heart from things that happened in the war are like the little piles of dirt Lucy swept under the rug. Just because you don't talk about them, don't bring them out where they can be seen, doesn't mean they are gone."

Daniel bristled. "No amount of talking is going to change anything, Mother."

"Maybe talking to us won't, but talking to God can." She gave his arm a little squeeze. "Give the hate to God, Daniel. All of it. It's the only way you'll ever get rid of it."

Mother finally slipped out of the door, and Daniel was glad. He had no intention of doing any more talking to God. He'd *been* talking to God and had gotten only heartache in return. Instead of talking, he'd like to rail at God for playing such a dirty trick on him. Of all the women who could have attached themselves to his heart, why this one?

What Charity told him should have killed any affection he had for her. But it hadn't. Instead it flourished, resisting his every effort to eradicate it. Her sweet, angelic face framed by honey-blond curls teased and tortured his every thought. Her visage vied with the gray, bloodied faces of Fred and Tom, their gory lips fashioning one accusing word, over and over.

"Traitor."

In Andersonville, the guards had mongrel dogs they abused in order to make them mean. When one dog would find a bone or morsel of food, another dog would grab the loose end in his mouth, and they'd snarl and fight until the prize was ripped asunder. Daniel felt as if there were two angry, fighting dogs inside him, pulling in opposite directions and ripping his insides to shreds.

He sank back to his bed. Bending forward, he pressed his face in his hands. Charity put him in Andersonville. But his love for her had sentenced him to a prison more awful than Andersonville—and one from which he feared he would never emerge.

twenty-two

"Write to 'im."

Charity looked up at Pearl from the library's mahogany desk top. "I will not!" She reared back in the leather chair as if the sheets of Aunt Jennie's stationery Pearl held out to her were red hot. "Have you lost your senses entirely, Pearl Emanuel?"

Pearl slammed the paper down on the desktop beside the mill's debit book. "Reckon I'm as sound in mind as most and better'n some!" Her dark eyes pinned Charity with a glare that dared her to break the gaze. "Adam said in his letter that Daniel's been mopin' aroun' like all the life's been plumb sucked outta him. Anyways, that's what Daniel's Aunt Rosaleen told Adam's ma."

"And why should I care in the least little bit if Daniel Morgan is mopin' or not?" Charity pretended to study numbers in the debit book, although her brain refused to register the figures on the page. As fond as she was of her friend, sometimes Pearl could irritate the hide off a mule!

"'Cause you love 'im."

At Pearl's quiet declaration, Charity puffed out a breath of surrender and grabbed the edge of the desk to help push herself up. She couldn't bear to hear the truth that screamed day and night from her heart put into words, even by Pearl, whom she loved like a sister.

She gingerly shifted her weight from her injured left leg. Although the leg grew stronger every day, she was still reluctant to exert much force on it. Last week, Dr. Morgan removed her splint, examined her leg, and declared her healed. Before he left, he apologized for his son's rude departure. He went on to explain that Daniel had been in the group of Union soldiers whose whereabouts Charity had alerted her brother to the day before the Battle of Peachtree Creek.

While Dr. Morgan's explanation had resolved the mystery of Daniel's sudden leave-taking, the implication of his words hit Charity like a body blow. Remembering how Asa had raced out of the house that day, she had no doubt her brother precipitated Daniel and the other Union soldiers' capture. That knowledge collided with the awful images of Andersonville Daniel had painted in her mind, making her physically ill.

Charity took a few halting steps toward the hat tree beside the library door that opened to the hallway. The day was unusually warm for mid-March, and if Pearl insisted on pestering her, she might as well enjoy the sunshine.

Pearl rounded the desk in pursuit. "Maybe you can run away from me, but you cain't run away from yer heart."

Charity reached for her shawl, then turned and gave Pearl a hug. "I know you mean well, but there's nothin' I can do or say to amend what I did." She shrugged her shoulders in defeat. "It doesn't matter how I feel about Daniel. He hates me—and I can't blame him."

"If he hated you, he wouldn't be mopin'." Pearl stepped between Charity and the doorway. "You got to tell him, Miss Charity. You got to tell him that you promised yer ma you'd take care of Asa an' you was feared Asa would run right smack into Daniel an' them other Yankee soldiers."

"Daniel doesn't care why I did it, Pearl. Andersonville crippled him and killed his friends."

Ignoring Pearl's scowl, Charity wrapped her shawl around her shoulders and limped out of the library, down the hall, and out of the front door.

Today, school was letting out for the summer, and in a half hour, Henry would be returning home. Dr. Morgan had suggested short walks would strengthen Charity's leg, and she knew it would please Henry for her to meet him at the crossroads of Jackson and Perry streets on the last day of school. Perhaps Pearl was right. Maybe she couldn't run away from her feelings for Daniel. But during the past week, she'd used her growing affection for Henry to help plug up the hole Daniel's leaving had gouged in her heart.

On the porch, she gripped the handrail alongside the two stone front steps and haltingly descended to the gravel walkway. It felt good to be outside again—to breathe in fresh air and feel the ground beneath her feet.

Beside the steps, she noticed yellow and purple crocuses blooming. Spring would come. Life would go on. Charity found little joy in the blossoms' silent proclamation.

She needed to get away—away from Vernon and the mill, places that evoked thoughts of Daniel. She was glad she'd saved the letter the New South Investment Company had sent to Sam. Tonight, she'd write to Mr. Armand Dubois and inquire if the land in Fulton County, Georgia, was still for sale.

Since the accident, the bond between Charity and Henry had grown even stronger. He increasingly looked to her as a mother figure, and she couldn't love him more if he was her natural son. Aunt Jennie and Uncle Silas had grown attached to the child as well, and Charity had no doubt Uncle Silas would be willing to become Henry's legal guardian.

But Henry needed a new start, too, and he still talked about returning to Georgia. Yesterday, Charity had read with interest an article in one of Aunt Jennie's penny magazines that told of churches recruiting missionaries to help with reconstruction of the South. They were especially looking for Christian teachers. She could join one of the groups traveling to Georgia. While there, she could search for any kin Henry might still have living in the state. It would also give her an opportunity to investigate the land New South Investment was selling in her home county. . . .

"Ah, Charity, ma chère. It is good to see you up and walking."

Annie Martin's voice filtered through Charity's musings.

Charity looked across the yard to where the old woman stood outside the front gate, a large market basket on her arm.

Annie grinned from the shaded depths of her dark wool bonnet. Her quick, studying gaze seemed to miss nothing as it slid over Charity.

"That evening last January down by the river, I wasn't sure I would see you again this side of heaven."

Charity limped toward the wrought-iron gate separating the two. "Now I distinctly remember you tellin' me I would be all right," she teased, responding with a grin of her own. Unlike Aunt Jennie or many of Charity's other female acquaintances, Annie would not take offense at such a contradictory rejoinder. Indeed, the sprightly old woman seemed to delight in friendly, verbal sparring.

"And so you would have been—either way." Annie's agate colored eyes sparkled and her chin lifted. "Like the Apostle Paul said, 'For to me to live is Christ, and to die is gain.' In Christ our souls are safe, wherever God decides they should dwell."

Charity gave a little laugh—the first that had passed her lips since Daniel left Vernon. Annie Martin was good medicine for her. "Of course you are right, Annie, as always."

Annie cast a glance across the street to the courthouse lawn. "I have been waiting all winter to sit on that bench beneath that old catalpa tree. Would you like to join me?"

Charity nodded. "I would love to." After weeks of Pearl and Aunt Jennie's doting, Annie's company was as refreshing as the spring breeze.

They ambled haltingly across Perry Street. Charity didn't doubt that the spry septuagenarian could have easily out-distanced her. But she appreciated Annie slowing her steps to accommodate Charity's infirmity.

They sat on the bench, and Annie placed her linen-covered basket on the spring grass at her feet. She reached beneath the linen cloth covering the basket and pulled out a square of blue knitting with two wooden needles attached. After a moment, she settled back against the bench and inhaled deeply. "Smell that? That's the smell of promise. . .of hope."

Charity followed her lead and sniffed the air filled with the earthy scents of sod, budding vegetation, and the unidentifiable fragrance of newness.

Sitting quietly with her hands clasped in her lap, Charity made no response. The words "hope" and "promise" held little meaning for her now. Those words had walked out of her life two weeks ago with Daniel.

"Funny how we're always surprised when they come back." Annie's words jerked Charity's attention back to the woman beside her.

"What?" Her mind never far from thoughts of Daniel, Charity's face warmed and her heart thumped harder.

"The spring bulb flowers." Annie nodded her bonneted head toward a row of little green spikes poking up along the base of the black iron fence. In another couple of weeks, the daffodils would decorate the fencerow with a solid line of sunny yellow blossoms. "Each spring, we're always just a little surprised to see them come up, do you not agree?"

"Yes, I suppose so," Charity mumbled. Her heart slowed to a more normal rhythm. She had no doubt that Annie was well aware Daniel had left Vernon. Little happened in this town that escaped Annie's knowledge. But Charity had just left the house to avoid a conversation with Pearl about Daniel. She had no interest in taking up the subject with Annie.

"It is like love, yes?" Annie gave her an innocuous smile as her nimble fingers worked the yarn around the clicking needles. "You may not see evidences of it for a season," she said, "but all things planted by God in the heart or in the earth do not die. They sleep and wait for God's hand to stir them awake, reviving our faith and reminding us that God, who makes all things new, is still in control."

Charity blinked back bitter tears. She understood Annie's little parable had to do with her heartbreak over Daniel.

When she could trust her voice, she faced Annie. "But if you dig up the bulbs—destroy them—they will not come back."

"Ahh." Annie stopped her work long enough to wave a wrinkled hand. "A few years ago, I dug up a clump of bluebells that grew behind my barn. I wanted to plant them instead under the tree by my front porch," she said with a grin. "I dug and dug and was sure I had them all."

Her fingers stilled again and the kind smile she turned to Charity smoothed the wrinkles around her mouth. "Yet every spring, bluebells still bloom behind my barn. We cannot destroy what God intends, ma chère."

Charity met her seatmate's knowing look, her eyes widening. Annie could not have known why Daniel left, yet somehow, the astute old woman must have guessed it had something to do with Charity.

They sat quietly for a time, watching robins peck for worms in the damp earth. Charity allowed the cheerful songs of the birds and the *clickety-click* of Annie's knitting needles to fill the silence that stretched between them.

"You do not believe me, ma chère?" Annie said at length, a smile embroidering the edges of her voice.

Charity shrugged. Let Annie think what she liked, but Charity had seen the look on Daniel's face before he walked out of her room that afternoon two weeks ago. Whatever love he'd had for her, she'd irreparably destroyed.

Charity rubbed her unadorned left hand and glanced at the little brick church perched on the hill above Jefferson Street, overlooking Vernon. Then her gaze slid to the large brick and stone courthouse to their right. If she had never forced that discussion with Daniel—if neither of them had learned of her part in his capture—the two of them might have been procuring their marriage license in that courthouse. Reverend Davenport might be performing their wedding ceremony. . . .

A renewed sense of loss seized Charity in an almost suffocating grip. The sooner she left Vernon, and Indiana, the better.

"I've decided to go back to Georgia," Charity blurted. "I thought perhaps I could search for some of Henry's kin. Uncle Silas and Aunt Jennie have been very generous concernin' Henry—as they have been with me—but if the boy has family there, it's only right that they learn of his situation." She fixed her gaze on a robin tugging a fat worm from the black earth but could feel the heat of Annie's scrutinizing gaze.

The clicking of Annie's needles slowed a beat or two. "It is a kind thing you and your kin did for the boy—taking him in. But from what I understand, the South is still very unsettled after the war. I would not have thought your aunt disposed to visiting a place in such turmoil."

Charity readjusted her shawl around her shoulders, wishing she had some knitting of her own to keep her hands busy. "My aunt and uncle and Henry won't be going. . .not at first, anyway. Just me."

Annie sat up straighter, and her knitting needles fell silent. "That is a long way for a young woman to go alone, do you not think, ma chère?"

A giggle burst from Charity's lips. A trip to Georgia paled in comparison to the harrowing stories Annie had told of her youth. "How can you say such a thing when you were dragged across the country by Shawnee during a war while in the family way?"

The clicking began again, and the smile returned to Annie's voice. "Well, it was not by choice. And I was only seventeen—too young to know just how frightened I should be. But you should know better than to travel alone—"

"But I won't be alone. I plan to join one of the missionary groups that are helpin' rebuild the South. I have an address of a group that is askin' for teachers to join them."

Annie's concerned scowl suddenly changed to one of startled

enlightenment. "Oh, I almost forgot." She dropped the knitting to her lap and reached into the basket. "That's what happens when you get old. You get forgetful," she added with a little laugh. "I stopped by the post office to mail a letter to my son Jonah and his wife, and Jim McClelland asked me to bring this by. He missed gettin' it in the bunch Pearl picked up earlier for you." She held out a little square envelope to Charity.

The sound of children's voices drew their attentions to the crossroads of Perry and Jackson Street. "Here comes your young charge now," Annie said.

Eager to reach Henry, Charity stuffed the envelope in her skirt pocket. The letter would have to wait. She rose stiffly, half wishing she had used the time to exercise her leg.

Annie grasped Charity's hand and angled her face up, her narrow auburn brows knitted together tighter than the rows of yarn she'd been working.

"Just be sure you're runnin' toward God's will and not away from it. Pray for God's guidance before you do anything, Charity. And give God time to do His work. *Qui vivra verra.* What will be, will be. But remember, 'A man's heart deviseth his way: but the Lord directeth his steps.'"

"I will pray, Annie," Charity promised. Eager to get to Henry and hear of his day, she slipped her fingers from the old woman's.

Annie's face brightened like the sky when the sun breaks through the clouds. "Thank you for keepin' me company for while. I think I'll sit here in the sun a bit longer and warm up like an old lizard on a rock," she said with a cackle.

With a parting smile and nod to Annie, Charity limped as quickly as her leg allowed toward Henry, who'd nearly reached the house. She would say nothing to him yet of her plans to travel to Georgia. She would take Annie's advice and pray about it.

But her heart wailed night and day in lament at the loss of Daniel's love. The only respite she could see was escape from this place and all that reminded her of him.

For some reason, God had seen fit to separate them with this unbridgeable chasm. Obviously, they were not meant to be together. Her only prayer now was that God would give her the courage to do what she needed to do for both her and Henry. And somehow, fill Daniel's heart with enough mercy that he wouldn't spend the rest of his life despising her.

That evening after supper, she passed the library and noticed Uncle Silas had left the light burning. Suddenly remembering the envelope Annie had given her, she reached into her pocket and pulled it out. When she examined the return address her heart raced. It was from Lucy Morgan.

Surely Lucy had learned of Charity's involvement in Daniel's capture. Could she be writing to vent her anger? The notion evaporated the moment it was formed. From what Charity had seen of Lucy Morgan, she doubted the woman capable of harboring even a speck of guile.

She broke the seal and slipped out the single sheet of fine stationery. Quickly perusing the missive, she realized it was an invitation to Lucy and Travis's wedding to be held in April the Saturday following Easter.

Beneath the formal invitation, Charity noticed Lucy had written a postscript.

> *I pray you will find it in your heart to grace us with your presence. Daniel's spirits have been so very low since returning to Madison, I am more than confident your attendance would be a positive tonic for his melancholy.*

The words blurred before Charity's misty eyes. Was Daniel grieving, too, over the lost joy they might have known together? Charity was not at all sure she shared Lucy's optimism. In all probability, her attendance would only serve to cause her and Daniel added pain.

On the other hand, perhaps this was an answer to her

prayer. She had no hope of reclaiming Daniel's love. But perhaps attending Lucy's wedding would provide her with an opportunity to beg his forgiveness, hopefully freeing both her and Daniel from a life sentence of anger and guilt.

twenty-three

"The whole family has gone mad!" Daniel muttered the sentiment he'd held for the past several days as he limped across the wide expanse of Main-Cross Street. Everyone but him, it seemed, was not only actively involved but obsessed with Lucy and Travis's coming wedding. As the date neared—now only two weeks away—the one advantage Daniel found amid the craziness was that the family's collective attention had shifted from him to his sister's nuptials.

Like a formidable army general, Mother led the campaign for a flawless wedding, daily assigning chores to each family member and household employee.

Daniel had no clue what errands Uncle Jacob had waiting for him at the church, but this morning when Mother consulted her wedding preparation notes and relegated errands, he welcomed the fact his assignment required a walk across town. After his discussion with mother concerning Charity, the sympathy heaped upon him had been next to smothering. So the mad dash to finalize the wedding plans had granted him a respite from his family's well-meaning, but exasperating pity.

However, Daniel's own mind and heart had not granted him any such respite. The sound of Charity calling his name as he walked away from her, down the Gants' staircase and out of the house, continued to echo torturously through his mind. The memory of the hurt tone in her voice slashed at his heart. He remembered the strong, painful tug on his heartstring that had momentarily halted his descent, urging him to turn back and retrace his steps. But pride? Anger? Perhaps both had propelled him down the stairs, out of Vernon, and out of her life.

More than once since his return home, he'd been tempted to gather up a few necessities and leave Madison—maybe even Indiana—and become the bummer Charity had accused him of being that first day at Gant's Mill. But deep down, he knew he could travel the world over and never escape his love for Charity Langdon. And that realization was gradually killing him.

He slowed his pace as he headed down Broadway. Easing down the sharp slope, he stretched out his longer leg first to accommodate his uneven gait. Thoughts of his own infirmity reminded him of Charity's injury. Was she walking now without the crutches he'd made for her? How carefully, how lovingly he'd fashioned those crutches. And when he'd presented them to her, his heart had swelled at the tears of appreciation he'd seen glistening in her blue eyes.

Daniel paused at the edge of Broadway while a wagon and mule team rumbled past, sending up gray puffs of gravel dust. He scrubbed his face. Then he remembered what Mother had told him and knew she was right. He could scrub his forehead raw and never erase the torturous images that lay behind it.

He gazed at the greening lawns coming alive with vivid colors of spring flowers. Yellow blooms covered the large Forsythia bush on the east side of Uncle Jacob and Aunt Rosaleen's parsonage. The cheerful chirping of birds tickled his ears. The scents of greening vegetation filled his nostrils. From every direction, the newness of spring bombarded his senses. It all felt like an insult to his withered spirit. Two weeks ago, his heart had blossomed like the burgeoning spring, joyfully anticipating joining his life with Charity's. But God had played a cruel trick, turning his sweet joy into souring resentment.

Daniel neared the church, not at all liking the wad of scorn and anger building inside him at the sight of the building. Uncle Jacob had helped to build this church with his own hands. Daniel had attended services here since the building's completion when he was six years old. It was in this church at the age of fourteen that he'd made his confession of faith and given his heart to Christ. Yet at this moment, as he gazed on the building's brick and stone façade, Daniel felt only anger.

Had he lost his faith entirely? Facing the enemy's rifles across the battlefields of the South, through the unspeakable horrors of Andersonville, when the *Sultana* hurled him into the Mississippi's unforgiving waters, he'd kept his faith. He'd clung to it like a lifeline. Even after the war when he'd ignored God, he'd felt no animosity toward his Maker.

But knowing that God had allowed him to fall helplessly in love with the woman who'd trespassed in the worst way against him and the men he'd loved like brothers was something he could not bear. He imagined the Almighty sneering down upon his misery, and a terrible, frightening rage boiled in his belly.

By the time he reached the church's steps, he had to summon every ounce of his sense of duty in order to mount them and enter the building. He'd come here to help Uncle Jacob, not to commune with God. The sound of wood clacking against wood greeted Daniel as he passed from the vestibule into the sanctuary.

Dressed in work trousers and rolled-up shirt sleeves, Uncle Jacob knelt on the raised stage at the front of the church prying up flooring planks with an iron crowbar.

Daniel made his way up the aisle between the rows of pews half wondering if his uncle had taken leave of his senses. "Uh, do you think it's a good idea to be tearing up the church just before Lucy's wedding—not to mention Easter?"

Uncle Jacob looked up and grinned. He ran the back of his hand across his sweaty forehead. "When that storm tore a hole in the roof last fall," he said glancing upwards, "rain damaged this floor. We had enough to do just getting the roof patched before winter. But now," he shifted his gaze down to the pile of ripped-up boards beside him, "this floor is beginning to warp." His grin widened. "I wouldn't want to be preaching—or about to proclaim your sister and Mr. Ashby man and wife—and suddenly disappear beneath the stage."

Chuckling at the picture, Daniel nodded and took in the situation. This was something he could do. The past two weeks of idleness had driven him to near distraction. He relished the opportunity to busy his hands working with tools and wood.

For the next several minutes, the two worked together with little talk. After determining the sub floor was undamaged, they began fitting new boards in place to close the gaping hole in the stage. Daniel picked up a fragrant, newly planed oak plank from the pile of replacement wood Uncle Jacob had assembled. Taking hold of one end while his uncle held the other, Daniel smacked the edge of the board with the heel of his hand, shoving it flush against the existing old flooring.

"Ouch!" Uncle Jacob shook his pinched finger then popped it into his mouth.

"Sorry, Uncle. I should have made sure your fingers were out of the way." Remorse smote him. Minor accidents were a common occurrence in woodworking, but he regretted that his inattention had caused his uncle an injury.

Uncle Jacob shook his head. "Don't wor—" He suddenly stopped and narrowed his eyes at Daniel. "What would you say if I said I don't forgive you for pinching my finger, Daniel?"

Bewildered and a little hurt, Daniel rocked back on his heels and met Uncle Jacob's look. It was not like his uncle to hold any kind of grudge, especially for something as trivial as a hurt finger.

Daniel gave a nervous chuckle. "I guess I'd say you need to get another helper."

"Of course I forgive you, Daniel." The kind smile Uncle Jacob gave Daniel swept him back to his childhood. "Do you feel better for having been forgiven?"

An uncomfortable feeling squiggled through Daniel. Exactly

what point was Uncle Jacob trying to make? "I suppose I do," he mumbled.

"And I feel better for having forgiven you."

Avoiding his uncle's gaze, Daniel lifted another new board from the pile beside them. "Is this one of your famous lessons, Uncle?"

Uncle Jacob gave a little shrug. "Just working out this Sunday's sermon. The theme is forgiveness and is taken from the fourth chapter of Ephesians. 'Let all bitterness, and wrath, and anger, and clamour, and evil speaking, be put away from you, with all malice: And be ye kind one to another, tenderhearted, forgiving one another, even as God for Christ's sake hath forgiven you.' I hope to show that by obeying Christ's commandment to forgive, both parties are blessed."

Daniel decided it might not be prudent to tell his uncle he didn't plan to be in the audience.

Uncle Jacob grunted and popped his finger into his mouth again. "Although forgiving you has lightened my soul, it's done nothing to stop this finger from bleeding," he said with a little laugh. "I'm afraid I'll have to have your Aunt Rosaleen bandage it. I'll be back directly." Stepping down from the stage, he headed toward the front door.

Daniel grinned. "I know you, Uncle. You just welcome an excuse for Aunt Rosaleen to dote on you."

"Don't need an excuse," his uncle shot over his shoulder before disappearing into the vestibule.

Daniel turned his attention back to the work at hand and pounded a nail into the new board, securing it to the sub-floor. Uncle Jacob was a wily old fox. He didn't doubt for a moment his uncle had the situation between Daniel and Charity in mind when he made the point about forgiveness.

Daniel blew out a deep breath and ran his hand over his face. After the war, he'd convinced himself he'd forgiven the Rebs for what they'd done to Tom and Fred. And to him. But he hadn't. Learning the part Charity had played in his capture had dredged up the foul, rotting hatred he'd buried in the dark recesses of his soul. Mother was right—simply not thinking about it didn't constitute forgiveness.

He pounded another nail into the board so hard the hammer's head dented the wood. He wasn't sure he *could* forgive his captors. Or that he wanted to.

And Charity shared their guilt. Her only thought had been to help the Confederacy, not caring what lives might be lost as a result. To continue loving her meant he had to forgive her. And forgiving her complicity in the matter felt dangerously close to treason. So somehow, some way, he had to stop loving her. And if that meant his soul must remain burdened, then so be it!

A sound near the vestibule yanked him from his troubling thoughts. Uncle Jacob must have returned. But when Daniel glanced up, he didn't see his uncle but was greeted instead by a dark, smiling face. For an instant, he thought it was Uncle Jacob's old friend, Andrew Chapman. But he quickly realized it was Pearl Emanuel's father, Jericho.

Daniel knew Uncle Jacob and Aunt Rosaleen enjoyed close acquaintances with the free blacks at Georgetown. He also suspected they remained deeply involved in the continued work of the Underground Railroad. He gave the man a smile and nod. "Jericho. If you'd like to talk to Uncle Jacob, he's gone to the parsonage. . . ."

Jericho shook his graying head as he continued walking toward the stage. "You's the one I wants to talk to, Mr. Morgan. Has to do with Miss Langdon."

Fear leapt in Daniel's chest. Strength drained out of him and he dropped the hammer with a clatter. Had something happened to Charity? "Is—is she ill? Is she hurt?"

Jericho shook his head, sending a wave of relief swooshing through Daniel. "My girl, Pearl, she writes reg'lar to Andrew Chapman's boy, Adam." He flashed a gleaming smile up to Daniel. "Pearl and Adam, they's promised, ya know."

Daniel nodded, wishing the man would get to the point.

"Well, sir. . . ," Jericho paused and twisted his black felt hat in his hand. As with many of his race who'd been reared in slavery, Jericho's gaze tended to slide downward when talking to white folks. "It ain't in my nature to interfere, but my girl begged me to talk to you. Seems Miss Charity's got a crazy notion in her head to go back to Georgia with a bunch o' missionary teachers 'n sich. The South ain't no safe place to be these days, Mr. Morgan."

Jericho's comment set Daniel back on his heels. But at second thought, he didn't find it all that surprising. He'd heard Charity mention on more than one occasion that she dreamed of returning to her home state. But Jericho was right. From what Daniel had heard, the South swarmed with carpetbaggers and rogues of every stripe. All points south of the Mason-Dixon Line were nearly as dangerous now as they'd been during the war.

As Daniel headed for the steps connecting the stage with the main sanctuary floor, one thought tamed the fear rearing up inside him. Silas and Jennie Gant would never agree to allow Charity to set off on any venture they'd deem unsafe.

Daniel settled himself on the top step and motioned for Jericho to join him. "Georgia? Surely Mr. and Mrs. Gant would never allow—"

"They don't know. Miss Charity made Pearl promise not to tell 'em." Jericho's jerky movements as he gingerly perched himself on the bottom step spoke of his unease. "But Pearl never promised not to tell anybody else. She thought maybe you—"

"I'm afraid Miss Langdon and I didn't part under friendly circumstances." Daniel's cheek twitched with the forced smile. Now it was his turn to feel uncomfortable.

"Pearl tol' me 'bout you bein' one of the soldiers Miss Charity saw at Peachtree Creek 'fore that battle in '64." For once, Jericho looked Daniel directly in the eye. "If you don't mind my sayin' so, I think there's somethin' you need to know."

Daniel cocked his head and sat up straighter, his spine stiffening. He wasn't sure he cared to hear any more about the incident, but he'd let the man have his say.

"Miss Charity—well, she feels like one of my own." Jericho's reddening eyes glistened with unshed tears. "Me'n Tunia, we b'longed to the plantation that bordered Miss Charity's pappy's place. We'd jist jumped the broom when the man who owned us took a notion to sell Tunia. Well, sir, Mr. Langdon got wind of it an' offered to buy us both. It liked to ruined him, but he done it." Jericho paused, cleared his throat, and dropped his gaze to his hands wadding his hat.

Daniel sat quietly, allowing the man to get a better grip on his emotions.

Jericho snuffed and swiped a weathered hand under his nose. "Miss Charity's pappy treated us more like fam'ly than slaves." He looked up at Daniel and flashed a grin. "We stayed, had our Pearl, and raised her 'longside Miss Charity and her brother, Asa. Then when Massa Langdon passed on, he left it in his will that we be freed. But we stayed and worked the mill, 'cause Miz Langdon was poorly and couldn'ta managed without us."

Although unsure what all this had to do with Charity's part in his capture, Daniel found the information fascinating and nodded for Jericho to proceed.

"Miss Charity, she was more like her pappy. Solid. Good head on her shoulders." He chuckled and shook his grizzled head. "That boy, though. . .he was a wild one. Wilder'n a deer. Always outta one scrape and into 'nother! After Massa Langdon passed on, it was all Charity's ma could do to keep that boy reined in. So when she knew she was 'bout to foller Massa Langdon through the pearly gates, she made Miss Charity promise to watch out for her brother—try to keep him safe."

Jericho's dark gaze pierced Daniel's. "That's what she was

tryin' to do that afternoon. Nothin' more. Nothin' less. Jist tryin' to do what she promised her ma." He shook his head sadly. "Didn't do no good though. Asa fell next day in battle, less than a half mile from where he was born and raised."

Daniel swallowed hard. He wouldn't have thought knowing the reason Charity had disclosed his and his men's location would make any difference to him. But it did.

With a groan, Jericho planted his hands against his knees and rose slowly. "Ol' bones don't move so fast these days," he said with a grin. "Sorry to take up so much of your time, Mr. Morgan." Then he narrowed his eyes at Daniel, his dark forehead wrinkling. "Jist thought you ought to know why she done it, that's all." He poked his chest with a finger. "Ain't never seen a better heart than what beats inside that girl." With that, Jericho turned and ambled down the aisle and out of the church.

The scripture Uncle Jacob had quoted about forgiveness talked about a tender heart. When Jericho explained Charity's actions, Daniel had felt his heart soften in his chest. He felt mean. Regret draped his spirit like a wet overcoat. If not for his capture, he would have participated in the Battle of Peachtree Creek. A minie ball from his own gun might have killed Charity's brother. How many times had he sighted down his rifle barrel at a faceless Confederate soldier, held his breath, squeezed the trigger, and watched his target fall lifeless before him?

Yet for the past two weeks, he'd done nothing but feel sorry for himself and rail at God like a sanctimonious idiot. The sour taste of hypocrisy rose up in his throat like bitter bile. How Charity must despise him—and he didn't blame her.

Daniel stood and gazed around this sanctuary he'd known since childhood. Why should he be surprised that it was in this place his heart finally heard the whisperings of God's still, small voice?

A new, terrible sadness took hold of him. It was too late. God had given him a chance to have Charity's love. And because he was too proud to forgive, he'd thrown it away. He wished with all of his heart he could do something to stop her from leaving for Georgia—to somehow protect her. But after walking away from her the way he did, he couldn't imagine convincing her to accept his apology, let alone to stay in Indiana.

He blinked back the emotion misting his sight. "Dear Lord, forgive me. I know I can never win back Charity's affection. I just ask that she not hold me in the basest contempt. And take care of her. Please, Lord, take care of her."

twenty-four

"I still think it's a bad idee!" Pearl huffed out the words as she walked beside Charity.

The considerable incline of Madison's Mulberry Street taxed Charity's lungs as well as her legs. Only now did she fully realize how much the weeks she'd spent convalescing in bed had weakened her constitution.

"I thought you wanted pearl buttons for your weddin' dress." Charity knew it was useless to act ignorant of Pearl's meaning, but she hoped to postpone the argument as long as possible. She wished now she hadn't told Pearl about the letter she received last week from Mr. Dubois, telling her of his plans to be in Madison.

"You know good an' well I ain't talkin' about shoppin' fer buttons." Pearl clutched Charity's arm to steady her when she stumbled slightly at a dip in the road.

"No good's gonna come from talkin' to that man. An' if Mammy knew we was goin' to that place, she'd rail and pray over us for two solid hours, then make us scrub with lye soap 'til our skin was raw!" A mixture of fear and aggravation flickered in Pearl's dark eyes. "In fact, I been prayin' the Good Lord'll send an angel to stop you right in yer tracks, 'cause heaven knows, I ain't been able to."

Charity stopped and drew in a restorative breath. She was glad they'd finally reached Main-Cross Street, but Pearl's words had dampened her earlier bravado. Indeed, she'd spent countless nights praying for God's guidance in the matter. But no good reason had presented itself to dissuade her from going forward with her plans.

"You act like it's a saloon or somethin', Pearl. It's just a hotel, and we'll only be in the lobby." She reached in her skirt pocket and fingered the letter she'd received two days ago from Armand Dubois.

"I jist don't like lyin' to Mammy. And that Madison Hotel is full of all kinds of dangerous gamblers an' such off them riverboats."

The quiver in Pearl's voice raked at Charity's conscience. Pearl and Adam's wedding was only two days away. She shouldn't be tarnishing her friend's joy with her own concerns.

Charity blinked back tears as she turned and gave Pearl a quick hug. She didn't like to think about starting a new life in Georgia without her childhood friend by her side. "We haven't lied to Tunia. We *are* goin' button shoppin'. Right after I talk to Mr. Dubois. And if you don't want to go in with me—"

Pearl gasped. "I ain't 'bout to let you go in the Madison Hotel by yerself! Hard tellin' what that carpetbagger and his scalawag friends might do!"

Charity turned her attention to the traffic along the main thoroughfare. She waited for a farm wagon and two buggies to pass, then started across the street's wide expanse. The sooner she got this meeting over, the better. "I'm just goin' to talk to Mr. Dubois about the land back home, Pearl. That's all."

Safely on the south side of Main-Cross Street, Pearl grasped Charity's arm and pulled her up short. "I ain't got a good feelin' 'bout this. 'Sides, you take off all sudden like an' you knows it'll throw Miz Jennie into all kinds o' conniptions an' vapors. Massa Gant won't have nobody to do all his mill figurin', an' it'll send poor li'l Henry into another fit o' grievin'."

Pearl's indictment rubbed sorely against Charity's raw conscience. Her aunt and uncle had been good to her. They'd taken her in and given her a nice life after she lost everything. And the way they'd accepted Henry after Sam's death had warmed her heart. She knew Pearl was right. Yet she couldn't turn her back on this chance to return to Georgia. . .and maybe find Henry's family in the bargain.

Charity pushed a long, weary sigh from her lips. "I promise I will tell them when I return to Vernon. The thought of hurtin' them truly pains me, but—"

"Charity? Why, it is you, isn't it?"

Lucy Morgan's voice spun Charity around. Heat filled her cheeks as she turned to face Daniel's sister. She hadn't replied to Lucy's wedding invitation, having not fully decided whether or not to attend the couple's nuptials.

The oversight seemed not to bother Lucy in the least. That musical little laugh Charity remembered bubbled from Lucy's lips as she trained her irrepressible smile on Charity. "I'm so glad to see you walking so well. I could hardly detect a limp."

Charity's burdened spirit lightened in the face of Lucy's infectious cheerfulness, and she experienced an unexpected flash of regret. It would have been nice to have this happy woman as a sister. She gave Lucy a heartfelt smile. "Please tell your father that I shall always be indebted to him for savin' my leg."

Lucy reached out and patted Charity's hand. She cocked her bonneted head, and her lips curved up gently. "Oh, what a sweet thing to say. Of course I will relay your sentiment to Papa. But just knowing that you are doing well is all the reward he requires." Then an impish grin replaced Lucy's kind smile. "Well, that and your uncle's generous payment of the bill," she added, sending out another melodic giggle to dance gaily on the spring air.

Lucy glanced down at the basket on her arm. "Speaking of financial matters—which I'm loath to do—I've just finished another shopping errand for wedding notions." Her slight shoulders rose and fell with her resigned sigh. "There seems to be no end to what a proper wedding requires, and the bills are adding up."

She grinned at Pearl. "At least I still have a week to prepare. I understand your big day is only two days away."

Eager to end the conversation and proceed on to the hotel

and her meeting with Dubois, Charity piped up before Pearl could answer. "Actually, Pearl and I are goin' shoppin' for buttons—for Pearl's weddin' dress." The half-truth chafed against Charity's conscience. But she couldn't very well divulge to Daniel's sister her other appointment.

Lucy gave a dismissive wave of her hand. "No need to buy buttons, Pearl. I bought far more buttons than I needed for my dress. You are welcome to as many as you'd like. Consider it an additional wedding present." Her azure eyes lit with rekindled enthusiasm. "Come, and I'll show you both my wedding dress while you pick out your buttons, Pearl."

Panic seized Charity. Her heart was not yet prepared to face Daniel. Perhaps when she'd solidified her plans to return to Georgia the thought of facing him would be less painful. "I—I don't know if we should—"

"Why, thank you kindly, Miss Lucy." This time it was Pearl who cut Charity off in mid-sentence. "Me an' Charity'd love to see yer dress. Wouldn't we, Charity?" Not allowing Charity the space of a half-breath to answer, Pearl turned back to Lucy. "I really appreciate you offerin' me the buttons. Like you said, the weddin' bills are addin' up." Pearl shot Charity a smug grin then stretched it into a brilliant smile which she slid toward Lucy. "You are an angel, and that's a fact, Miss Lucy."

Outnumbered, Charity cast a longing glance toward the Madison Hotel. According to Armand Dubois' letter, he should be in Madison for the next couple of days. There would be ample opportunity to meet with him.

But as Pearl dragged her down the boardwalk behind Lucy Morgan, Charity knew the quivering inside her had little to do with missing her appointed meeting with the carpetbagger. It had everything to do with the probability of another meeting—one she dreaded.

ॐ

Daniel pulled on the reins to slow the pair of horses as he neared the intersection of Main-Cross and Mulberry Streets.

Ignoring angry comments by drivers forced to maneuver around him, he brought the team and wagon to a complete stop.

He glanced northward where Mulberry sloped gently downward toward Georgetown. The war Jericho Emanuel's words loosed inside him last week raged more fiercely. According to Aunt Rosaleen's friend and housekeeper, Patsey Chapman, Charity had come to Madison to attend Adam Chapman and Pearl Emanuel's wedding.

The muscles in Daniel's arms twitched, wanting to turn the wagon toward Georgetown. How many times in the past week had he started to the train depot to buy a ticket to Vernon, only to turn around and walk back to the house?

He scoured his face with his hand. What would he say if he did confront Charity? Would he beg her forgiveness for walking away from her like a cad and a coward? Would he demand she not leave Indiana for Georgia? Would he warn her of the dangers she might face traveling alone to the South?

And if he did, how would she respond? Daniel was sure he knew. In his mind's eye, he'd seen it played over and over in excruciating repetition. She'd laugh in his face—a sour, scoffing laugh. Then, she'd gore him with a glare sharper than any bayonet and demand he remove his pitiful Yankee carcass from his sight.

At least that was the response he expected—the response he knew he deserved.

And even if he did manage to screw up his courage enough to beg her forgiveness and attempt to persuade her from leaving, what would it accomplish? It would only make her hate him even more. If that was possible.

He despised his cowardice. Even though he deserved them, he dreaded the thought of experiencing Charity's scathing recriminations.

Daniel snapped the reins down sharply against the horses' rumps, causing them to bolt. The wagon lurched down Main-Cross Street, and he pressed the soles of his boots hard against the angled footboard to steady himself. As the wagon bounced over the gravel street toward home, he gripped the leather lines so tightly his fingers cramped.

With effort, he forced his thoughts from Charity and back to the errands Mother and Lucy had assigned to him for the day. Later this afternoon, he would need to fetch Aunt Susannah and Cousin Georgiana from the depot when their train arrived from Indianapolis.

Daniel parked the wagon in front of the house and climbed down. At least the endless tasks preparing for his sister's wedding helped to fill his days and offer a diversion from agonizing over Charity. He didn't care to think beyond Lucy's wedding.

❧

Charity stood transfixed in Mrs. Morgan's upstairs sewing room. Her gaze refused to budge from the breathtaking beauty of Lucy's wedding dress. Displayed on a dressmaker's form, the frock was a full-skirted vision of pale ivory silk satin overlaid with Honiton and net bobbin lace. It shimmered with hundreds of crystal and mother-of-pearl beads that adorned its V-shaped neckline, elbow length sleeves, and voluminous skirt.

Moments ago, Charity and Pearl had literally gasped with awe when Lucy carefully removed the protective sheet from the dress. But they'd barely gotten a glimpse when Mrs. Morgan appeared in the open doorway. Apologizing for the interruption, she'd requested Lucy's help with something in the kitchen. She also informed Pearl that Patsey Chapman, Pearl's future mother-in-law, had stopped by and would like a word with her.

Tears dimmed the wedding gown's glory. Charity couldn't help imagining herself wearing this beautiful creation and standing beside Daniel as they exchanged marriage vows.

She blinked back her tears and turned to the button box Lucy had placed on a little round table. That dream had died when Daniel walked out of her sickroom three weeks ago.

She'd been relieved to learn from Lucy that he was out on an errand and wasn't due back for another hour. Hopefully, she would be gone long before he returned.

The sound of footsteps on the stairs buoyed that hope and she reached for the button box. The sooner Pearl chose the buttons for her dress, the sooner they could leave.

"Lucy, what time did you say Aunt Susannah's train is due in at the depot?" Daniel's voice shot through Charity like a lightning bolt.

Charity's heart bounced painfully against her ribs. She whirled toward the open door and dropped the button box, scattering its contents over the room's floral carpet.

For a long moment they just stood staring at one another across the threshold.

Daniel's dark eyes were as wide as silver dollars in his pale face, and his unshaven jaw hung slack.

Charity suspected her expression mimicked his.

"I'm sorry." They said the words in near unison, and incredibly, Daniel's eyes grew even larger.

Frozen in place, Charity felt powerless to move. In almost detached fascination, she watched his Adam's apple bob in his throat as he stepped into the room.

The afternoon sun slanted through a long window on the west wall and glinted on his raven-black hair. It reminded Charity of that first day he entered her uncle's mill last August. He was dressed much the same—a faded blue shirt, rolled up at the elbows, and black cotton work trousers.

He took another couple of steps toward her, and her heart crimped at his halting gait. Seven weeks ago, she'd begun dreaming of becoming his wife. She remembered how she'd smiled, imagining them limping together down the aisle of the little brick church in Vernon.

Amazingly, Daniel reached out and took both of her hands in his, sending a jolt through her body. His eyes, now hooded with a look of pain, glistened with unshed tears. "I'm sorry. I'm so sorry, Charity."

His unbelievable words jarred her free from her paralyzed state. Why on earth was he apologizing when it was she who'd injured him?

"Sorry for what?" Charity reared back but allowed him to keep her hands captive in his.

A bewildered frown wrinkled his broad brow. "For walking away from you—from us—like the cad and coward I am."

Images of unspeakable suffering her actions had brought upon Daniel flashed in Charity's mind. Shame seared her soul, and her heart throbbed with an unfathomable, aching love. "It is I who should be beggin' your pardon." Charity allowed the tears to stream unmolested down her face. "If I hadn't told Asa—"

Daniel shook his head, and his strong fingers gripped hers tighter. "Jericho told me. . .about the promise you made to your ma. I have no right to fault you for trying to save your brother." The corner of his mouth jerked in a failed attempt at a smile. "I thank the Lord I was not allowed to take part in that battle at Peachtree Creek. I don't have to wonder every day for the rest of my life if it was my bullet that—"

"Oh, Daniel!" The agony in Daniel's voice was more than Charity could bear. She threw herself against his chest and sobbed. "Please forgive me. Please say you forgive me."

"I forgive you, my love. I forgive you," he murmured against her hair. "Do you forgive me for walking out on you like a coward?"

A burst of indignation pushed her away from the sweet sanctuary of his embrace. She lifted a stern face to his. "You are not a coward, Daniel Morgan, and I won't allow anyone— not even you—to say you are! You are my good, sweet Daniel. The man I love."

Suddenly, his arms tightened around her, his head lowered, and his lips captured hers. The world could have crumbled around her and Charity wouldn't have cared. At last, she knew she was where she belonged—where she needed to be for the rest of her life.

Without warning, Daniel released her and dropped to one knee. Keeping her hands in his, he gazed up at her, his dark eyes glistening. "Charity Langdon, I told you once, and I'll tell you again. You've owned my heart since last August. Will you put me out of my misery and agree to be my wife?"

A deluge of new tears washed down Charity's face. Her head bobbed with fierce nods until she finally managed to push the word between her sobs. "Yes."

A twittering sound near the door intruded into their private island of happiness. Lucy's voice, embroidered with her sprite laugh, skipped into the room. "Well don't stay down there like a dunderhead, Daniel! Get up and kiss her!"

And so he did.

epilogue

"We'll miss you." Uncle Silas's gruff voice in the little foyer was thick with emotion, and his eyes glistened with moisture.

Charity reached up on tiptoes and kissed his weathered cheek above his grizzled beard, then patted his arm linked with hers. "We will just be in North Vernon, Uncle Silas. And since you've made Daniel part owner in the mill, we'll both be seein' you there nearly every day."

He cleared his throat. "Still, it will be different."

Surprised at her uncle's display of sentimentality, Charity couldn't help a giggle. "Remember, you and Aunt Jennie will have Henry for the first month while Daniel and I settle in. I have no doubt he will be company enough."

Remorse smote Charity's conscience. Pearl's assessment had been right. If God had not intervened and changed Charity's plans, her leaving would have indeed shattered her aunt's and uncle's hearts. It seemed incredible that only three weeks ago, God had reached down, saved her from her folly, and shifted the course of so many dear lives.

She suddenly remembered her missed meeting with Armand Dubois and had to suppress a giggle. After Daniel's marriage proposal, she hadn't given the carpetbagger another thought. It tickled her to imagine his continually checking his watch while pacing and fuming in the lobby of the Madison Hotel.

None of that mattered now. Here in the foyer of the little church overlooking Vernon, Charity's heart was at peace. Her future sparkled like the morning sun glinting off the myriad beads that adorned her wedding dress—the same dress her future sister-in-law wore two weeks ago to wed her dear Travis.

The first strong notes of "Blest Be the Tie That Binds" filtered into the foyer, sending nervous butterflies flitting in Charity's stomach.

She tightly gripped her nosegay that silently exclaimed, in the language of flowers, all the emotions throbbing in her chest. Deep purple violets spoke of her undying love and faithfulness, wild yellow irises proclaimed her faith in God and hope for future happiness, while sprigs of yarrow pledged final healing of all past wounds. Glancing down at the faded ribbons that bound the bouquet, she was struck by their symbolism as well. Violet ribbons from Daniel's mother's wedding bonnet twined with the yellow ribbons Mamma had worn in her hair when she married Papa. Two families, one from the North and one from the South, were uniting. Perhaps, in some small way, she and Daniel were part of God's larger plan to heal the nation.

As Uncle Silas escorted her into the sanctuary and down the church's center aisle to where her darling waited, all other thoughts fell away.

Daniel took her hands in his, enfolding them in his warm, strong fingers.

As they pledged their vows to one another, his dark gaze melting into hers held no hint of regret or lingering rancor. Only love.

And when the Reverend Davenport pronounced them man and wife, Charity could almost feel God fusing her and Daniel's hearts and spirits into one.

The soft whispering of her mother's voice filtered through the celebration of joy bursting inside Charity.

"And now abideth faith, hope, charity, these three; but the greatest of these is charity."

At last, she understood the full meaning of that scripture and the power of God's grace and forgiveness.

As her husband bent to brush a tender kiss across her lips, a bevy of grateful prayers lifted heavenward from Charity's heart.